There they were, ~~soaking~~ up the hot Mexican sun, looking like three rich American tourists. Bobby Cassiopea, Lou Scapelli, and Eduardo Fulgencio. Decorating their lush poolside patio were six gorgeous gals in brief bikinis and a white suited servant. Life was good for the boys here in Acapulco. But in a few minutes they'd be ready for giant plastic baggies. Three Mafia corpses for the next flight home. As baggage.

A half-mile away, studying the triple target through a high-powered gun scope was Mack Bolan. The range was 700 meters. The wind was from the southeast at ten knots. A tricky shot in any man's book. Marksmanship was talent plus a mastery of detail, and an intuitive ability to eliminate error. Bolan had counted down to zero, and was now centering the crosshairs on the final target ... it was as simple as 1, 2, 3.

The next target would be Bolan. Not so simple.

The Executioner Series:

the EXECUTIONER
ACAPULCO RAMPAGE

by Don Pendleton

PINNACLE BOOKS   NEW YORK CITY

For my ladies;
God love them all.

dp

This is a work of fiction. All the characters and events portrayed in this book are fictional, and any resemblance to real people or incidents is purely coincidental.

THE EXECUTIONER: ACAPULCO RAMPAGE

Copyright © 1976 by Pinnacle Books, Inc.

An original Pinnacle Books edition, published for the first time anywhere.

ISBN: 0-523-00868-6

First printing, June 1976

Cover illustration by Gil Cohen

Printed in the United States of America

PINNACLE BOOKS, INC.
275 Madison Avenue
New York, N.Y. 10016

Your message I hear, but faith
  has not been given;
The dearest child of Faith is
  Miracle.

     —*Goethe*

If I can't kill them, maybe
I can convert them.
If I can't convert them, maybe
I can at least induce belief.
In the end, though,
I will probably have to kill them all.
And that could take a miracle.

    —*Mack Bolan*
     (*from his* Journal)

Table of Contents

Prologue

"I will shake their house down!"

So declared the young sergeant fresh from Vietnam, at the beginning of his homefront war against the Mafia. He had not, however, expected to shake the entire world. In that beginning, the organized underworld lay at Sgt. Bolan's own doorstep—localized there, in his awareness, as the visible tip of an iceberg and personalized there in the untimely deaths of his mother, father, and kid sister.

Yeah, he would shake their house down.

From within, as it were, even while knowing that the collapse of that putrid structure would undoubtedly bury him in its debris.

But it did not bury him. Mack Bolan emerged from the ruins of the Pittsfield house of Mafia a bit wiser, a whole lot stronger, and totally dedicated to a war unto death. The only uncertainty seemed to lie in the question of who would be the first to die: Mack Bolan or the Mafia? And even that very basic question seemed to be purely rhetorical. The odds were overwhelmingly against the one-man army. The Mafia was a very old idea . . . and a very strong one. Their numbers were legion, their influence all-pervasive, their power seemingly unlimited. Their "friends"—*amici di l'amici*, friends of the friends—were everywhere in positions of quiet power: as cops, judges, legislators, politicians of every stripe and station, bureaucrats, businessmen—kingmakers and moneymakers, wherever the dollar was God and power was the key to the kingdom.

A worried U.S. attorney general had already conceded the existence of "an invisible second government" when Mack Bolan declared his war without end upon this twentieth-century version of the powers of darkness. The national infrastructure became quickly apparent to Bolan himself. The "House of Mafia" became a palace of many rooms, an international house with a maze of corridors stretching across all boundaries of geography and politics and reaching into every nook and corner of the civilized world.

"Today Pittsfield, tomorrow the world," might well have been Mack Bolan's battle cry in that beginning. Except that he was not a comic-strip hero, some sort of superman. He was not all-knowing, all-wise, all-powerful. He bled, like other men—knew fear and self-doubt, like other men—made mistakes, like other men.

"I will shake their house down!" was his promise to himself. He had not known, though, the dimensions of that house. He had not been aware of the fullness and complexity of its design, the foundations of its many rooms nor the directions of its endless corridors.

At Pittsfield, Mack Bolan made a promise to himself—and to his beloved dead. And then he began to understand what it was he had promised.

He had promised to shake the world.

So, okay—he would do that, too. If he could.

1: Bone Yard

The range was 700 meters—or a little more than a half mile. The big Weatherby .460 was the natural choice of weapons, blowing a muzzle energy of more than 8,000 foot-pounds to propel a heavy 500-grain bullet along that three-second course.

At such a range, the impact velocity would fall to something like a thousand feet per second. For this reason, he'd selected a controlled-expansion Nosler partition bullet for sustained penetration during expansion—he was going for bone, not mere flesh—for a sure kill, not a medical challenge.

This punch needed to be quick, stunning, *shaking*!—enough so to propel hardened men into panicky reaction—enough to put the fear of judgment into those who'd long thought themselves above any such mortal measurements.

The one under measure at the moment was smiling into the crosshairs of the high resolution sniperscope, apparently a contented man with nothing on his mind more pressing than the question of which tantalizing woman to lie down with next—or whether to take her beside the pool or in the water in an Acapulco crawl.

Sure, the guy had it made. That lazy smile which nearly filled the 20-power field of vision told it all. One of the golden ones, a super-*macho* of the jet set, whiz kid of the world money markets, confidant of the power elite. Yeah, this guy had it made. So big, and so well made, that he'd earned a code name—"Butch Cassidy"— from the feds who'd been trying to nail him all these years. Real name: Bobby Cassiopea. Real occupation: laundryman for dirty money. Real affiliation: *Mafia*.

Once written up in a national magazine as "the playboy financier of the Western world," the guy was a representative sample of the rapidly emerging new look in international hoods—suave, educated, untainted by overt association with known criminals but covertly as savagely rapacious as any street soldier and probably more so. More dangerous, certainly. This type dealt in *big* misery. And yeah, Bolan knew Bobby Cassiopea. The guy consorted with sheiks and prime ministers, Zurich bankers and Monte Carlo high-rollers, multinational tycoons and movie queens.

Cassiopea was, in mob language, "a natural." He was also a nobody, a nonperson in the invisible second government of the world. The mob owned him, body and soul. They'd raised him, educated him, financed him and arranged a "marriage of convenience" with an Italian noblewoman, which provided him social station and worldly visibility. The guy was a walking and talking fabrication, a "dummy" for the wiseguys who sat behind the curtain and pulled his strings.

But, sure, Cass Baby had it made. There was something essentially sad in that. A ghetto kid killing time on a street corner owned more than this guy did. A made man could never claim his own soul. Not while he lived.

Bolan shrugged away the thought as the Weatherby swung gently on the tripod and another face moved into focus—this one more at home on a movie or television screen—fiftyish, puffed and lined with the dissipations of a life too eagerly spent, still handsome and probably still capable of producing pitty-pats in a few million female hearts. The one and only John Royal. Bolan knew the gentleman by reputation only, and it was a mixed and questionable bag.

He sighed and continued to scan. Lou Scapelli and Eduardo Fulgencio, the Central American junkmen, completed the set at poolside—discounting the six bikini-clad decorations scattered about on sunning boards. A servant in white uniform stood unobtrusively at a small bar in the background. A couple of the girls were sucking separate straws and sharing a *coco preparado*, a local favorite featuring gin in a green coconut. Fulgencio had a beer; the other men were toying with highball glasses.

7

Two guys in swim trunks and brightly colored shirts patrolled the beach below the pool area. Another remained with the boat which had brought Scapelli and Fulgencio to the Royal villa for the poolside parley.

So the range was 700 meters and the stage was set. Bolan grimaced and consulted the trajectory graphs for the Weatherby, then ran a wind calculation.

It could be a tricky shot. The wind was coming over his right shoulder at about four o'clock, steady at about ten knots. This was on the heights, though. Something of a swirling effect was evident down there at target zone. Marksmanship was a science, sure, but the mathematics could take a guy just so far. Then the principle of uncertainty took over, increasing proportionately to the distance traveled. An error of only one-twelfth minute of angle—at this range and with the uncertain wind situation—could translate into a target error of a foot.

Bolan could not tolerate that degree of error.

He wanted headbone. He wanted it surely and methodically.

Good marksmanship, in the final analysis, becomes a matter of almost supersensory "feel." A guy took care of his mathematics and worked them to the finest point. Only "feel" or luck could carry across the zone of final uncertainty. And the Executioner could not afford to rely on mere luck.

He quickly double-checked the ballistics con-

8

siderations, then went through the target zone choreography. The sound wave would ride in with the bullet, or no more than a step behind. The reaction down there would be immediate and instinctive.

The marksman projected himself into that target zone and into each target, reading the physical layout and the most likely instinct path for targets two and three.

So, yeah ... allow two seconds for realization, another second for galvanization and full flight to cover.

Scapelli was small, nervous, quick. He'd take off running—probably heading for the patio wall, twenty paces away. A scared man could cover a lot of ground in three seconds—and that was about all the guy would have. Bolan gave him ten paces, and marked the spot.

Fulgencio was a heavy, ponderous man. He would opt for lighter cover, closer. The pool. Bolan traced the shortest path and marked the intercept point on that route, then concentrated fully on the windage problem.

Two clicks adjustment into the wind, and he was ready.

The Weatherby was ready, with one massive round in the chamber and two more in the magazine. And the target zone was ready.

The one and only John Royal was not a target—not this time around anyway. He was leaning back in his chair, signaling for the barman. No problem there.

Cass Baby was semireclining on his chaise longue and smiling at something being told him by Scapelli. Full face front, no likelihood of lateral displacement ... target positive.

The "horse master" himself was bent forward at Cassiopea's right, feet flat on the ground, talking with a lot of hand motion and really into what he was saying. Target probable for running intercept.

The Honduran, Fulgencio, was seated crosswise on a sunning board, sucking beer and staring with undisguised interest at the thong-bikinied sunbathers, who were nowhere near the target zone. His expression seemed to be saying: "Let's get this over with and get the broads over here." Target positive for scrambling intercept.

Bolan was in firing prone, at an elevation of several hundred feet above the target zone. From his position, he could view the full sweep of Acapulco Bay and follow the Costera Miguel Aleman, the bay drive, from Gran Via to Guitarron Beach. It was a stunningly scenic panorama—too beautiful, really, for the grisly events unfolding in its midst.

But, then, there were those cannibals down there, you see ...

Bolan grimaced and sent his mind back to his work.

The crosshairs took station on the base of Cass Baby's nose. The superb marksman took a long, measured breath and let half of it out, then sighed an audible "One" as he squeezed into the pull.

The big piece thundered into the recoil as he grimly rode it at the proper eye relief to get impact verification—reacquiring target on the four-count and just as the 500-grain Nosler reached destination. It smacked in just above the right eye. The rest of that once-handsome head seemed to collapse around that point, the smiling face contorting into a destruct-grimace, the entire field of vision instantly converting to a red froth as Target One disappeared from view.

Bolan was still counting as the crosshairs swept on, past blurred images of energetic motion. He reached Mark Two on the six-count and squeezed off again, firing at nothing more than a mental mark on a wall—then again quickly working the bolt and tracking on to Mark Three. But then a subliminal quiver of psyche stayed that round; he tracked quickly back along the instinct path and picked up his target.

Basic miscalculation, yeah.

The fat man was on all fours, crawling slowly and hesitantly toward the pool, dragging the overturned sunning board along with him. Some cover. A couple inches of expanded plastic or plexiglas.

Bolan corrected two clicks right, set the crosshairs squarely on target, and let it fly. The big bullet crunched in precisely three numbers later and dead on, punching through the flimsy barricade and finding head at kill velocity.

The Executioner lifted off the weapon and used the big four-inch spotting scope for target zone evaluation. The still form of Bobby Cassiopea was lying facedown beside an overturned longue. Lou Scapelli lay in a grotesque sprawl near the patio wall, right arm jerking spasmodically, bleeding from the mouth. Sloppy hit. It had caught him in the back, between the shoulder blades. Eduardo Fulgencio had died at mid-crawl and curled into a fetal ball; the top of his head was missing, the brain exposed and leaking.

John Royal was standing woodenly beside his chair, staring uncomprehendingly down upon the still form at his feet. The barman had come unglued and was beginning to move slowly toward his employer. The girls were just beginning to understand what had happened and were scrambling together for safety.

The two beach guards were nowhere to be seen. The other guy was apparently in the water, alongside his boat.

So okay. He'd given them a boneyard to contemplate—and apparently he'd stunned them. Another twenty or thirty seconds and the mood down there would shift into another gear. It remained to be seen whether or not he'd managed to shake anything loose.

He gathered the expended cartridges and formed a little triangle with them on the ground, then added a marksman's medal to the design. They'd find it. And they'd know.

Thirty seconds later, he was stowing his gear

in a candy-striped jeep and pitching his mind to the next point of contact.

Yeah. Very quickly now, they would know that a war had come to Acapulco.

2: The Rattle

It was unbelievable ... some kind of crazy dream. One moment they'd been having a friendly drink over a casual business meeting. The next moment *this*! For God's *sake*!

Royal shuddered and scrubbed frantically with a napkin at the spatterings on his own face and arms then took a quick step away from the flow of blood advancing upon his feet from the shattered head of Bobby Cassiopea.

He dropped the napkin over that unsettling mess and shakily lit a cigarette, trying to collect himself and sending an unblinking gaze across to the huddle of stunned women. He reacted with a start to the sudden appearance of the Mexican barman at his elbow.

"The gringo is dead, señor?" the barman inquired in a funeral-parlor voice.

"You better believe it," Royal grunted, between pulls at the cigarette. "Take the ladies inside, will you, Jorge? But keep them here. Don't let anybody leave."

The head of one of the beach guards appeared at the wall as the barman moved woodenly across the patio. The guard's eyes did a double take on the human litter scattered there.

"You okay, Mr. Royal?"

"Yeah. I guess so. Would you look at this mess? Would you look at it?"

The guard was looking at it, all right.

Mere seconds had elapsed since Cass's head had disintegrated right before John Royal's eyes. He had not even seen the hits on the other two.

Crazy, yeah. Unbelievable. Incredible. It didn't happen this way, did it? Not in real life.

The barman was herding the girls into the house.

Both security men were now scrambling over the patio wall from the beach and moving warily toward the victims.

Incredible!

"This one's alive, Mr. Royal . . . but just."

The guy was crouched over Scapelli. The actor winced at that news. It was easier to accept a dead gangster on his patio than a grievously wounded one.

"This one's gone," was the other report. "Brains and all."

Cut and print. It's a wrap.

Why not? Wasn't that the way it was usually done? Then the victims got up and had a chummy drink with their assassins.

It's not a movie set, JR. You can't wrap this one.

No? Why not?

"We better get an ambulance, Mr. Royal."

That's why not.

"You crazy?" Royal growled at the guard. "He'd be DOA, anyway. Look, I've got no stake in any of this. I want these guys out of here. Put them on the boat."

"I'm not getting paid to bury bodies at sea, sir."

Unbelievable! Wake up, dammit—wake up!

"You are now," Royal heard himself replying to the reluctant accomplice. "Get to it. I have to call the Man." He turned dazed eyes from the scene of carnage and lurched toward the house.

"It'll cost you a thousand for each of us, sir—with or without the Man."

Royal whirled about, arm outstretched at shoulder level, punctuating his angry words with a stiffly jabbing forefinger. "It will cost *you* your fucking *head* if you *don't*!"

He went blindly on, then, to the door and stepped inside.

What the hell! He hadn't asked for any of this. It was *his* villa, dammit—*his*, not the *Man's*. Keep the goddam garbage where it belonged. He didn't need it here.

The "ladies" were sprawled about in little islands of gloom. One of them was bawling—for what possible reason, Johnny Royal could not fathom. The others simply appeared frightened,

16

thoughtful—perhaps with the same sobering thoughts now occupying Royal's own mind.

The starlet of the moment, Angie Greene, placed a hand on his arm as he tried to brush by, fixing him with a solemn eye.

"What happened out there, Johnny?" she asked calmly.

"Why ask?" he growled. "You saw the same thing I did."

"I saw nothing," she told him in that same controlled soundstage voice.

"Just remember that," he said, and went on to the telephone.

Christ! How long had it been? A minute? No more than two, for sure.

He got his connection and spoke coolly into it. "This is JR. Tell the Man."

"It's me, Johnny. What's happening?"

"I thought maybe you'd tell me, Max."

"You talking about the gunfire?"

"You heard it?"

"Hell, I guess the whole damn bay heard it. Sounded like it came from up above the Holiday Inn, somewhere there. You worried about it?"

"No, I'm not worried about it, Max. I'm stuck with it."

"What d'you mean?"

"You better get over here."

"Tell me what you're talking about, Johnny."

"Your meeting dissolved, Max. Three claps of the gavel, and it's all gone to hell. Cass and the horsemen, they all got it."

17

"That's crazy, Johnny. Those shots came from a mile away."

"They got here, Max. Now I think *you'd* better get here."

"Give me five minutes. Don't call nobody else. You know?"

"I know, Max. God's sake, just come."

He hung up and went over to take the drink which the barman had been carrying since the shooting began.

"Nothing happened here, Jorge."

"Okay. It did not happen, Señor Royal."

"*What* didn't happen?"

"Nothing didn't happen, señor."

"That's right. Angie!"

"Right here, Johnny."

"Take the girls skiing. Use the outboard."

"Right."

"Angie!"

"Uh huh?"

"Tell the girls what Mexican jails are like. Tell them about the Napoleonic Code. Tell them how nice it is in a country like this to keep their goddam jaws wired shut. Tell them about the Man."

"I'll clue them in," she promised, and began moving the beauty parade outside.

God's sake! How had he ever allowed himself to be *used* like this? God's sake! Shots heard around the bay, garbage on his patio, the whole goddam . . .

No way, baby!

18

The whole thing smelled, it stunk. If Max was behind this, if he'd set up this whole thing—God, what if he had!

Royal hurried to the door and yelled to the men outside, "Forget it! Let them lie! Max can handle his own garbage!"

He staggered into the bathroom, still slightly dazed and fuming over unthinkable thoughts, to wash the traces of gore from his face and hands—then decided he'd better change his clothes, also. Even his shoes were spattered with Cass Baby.

Moments later, when Max and his retinue of torpedoes made the scene, JR was back in the saddle again and ready for the worst. He greeted them with a lukewarm smile and told the Man, "By the pool. I don't appreciate this, Max. I think it stinks."

"We'll see," Max replied coldly, and led his boys to the patio.

They swarmed it, like so many angry bees on territorial patrol, calling terse comments to one another and comparing findings.

"Did you move them?" the Man wondered aloud to JR.

Royal shot a quick look at his beachmen before replying to that. "I thought about it. Naw. That's where they fell."

Too Bad Paul, the crew boss, made a funny sound in his throat. He was squinting toward the heights, up-beach.

Max looked at his crew boss and said, "Yeah. Figure that, Too Bad."

"Did you set this up?" Royal demanded, his anger surfacing.

"Almost wish I had," the Man replied, sighing. "What do you make it, Too Bad?"

"One, two, three," the big guy growled. "Cass first—caught him dead in his chair. Then Scapelli—knocked him off his running feet. Then Fats. He had 'em snockered. The hit on Scapelli is unbelievable—maybe pure luck. He was running *across* the zone, just like he should've been. The guy would've had to have led him by a yard to make that hit."

"Who d'you know around here can shoot like that?"

"Nobody."

"Okay. Let's find the drop."

Royal watched with growing squeamishness as the torpedoes righted the chaise longue and lifted the ghastly corpse onto it. They fussed with the positioning of the body and demanded Royal's cooperation toward a reenactment. He grudgingly cooperated, and even told them about the spray of life fluids which had showered him with dying debris.

One of the men set up a gadget which looked like a surveyor's theodolite and began "shooting angles" from each of the victims.

At that point, Royal confided to the Man, "Uh, Max, Scapelli didn't die right away. I don't know if that means something."

"It means you used your head," Max replied coolly.

"Well, I didn't know. I just didn't . . ."

"You did okay. Don't worry about any public embarrassment, Johnny. We'll take care of all that."

"Oh, sure, I knew you would. I hardly knew these guys, Max."

"Don't worry about it. We'll take care of it. You just mind the store. Uh, how many witnesses we got here, Johnny?"

"Just, uh, Jorge and me. The beach boys. The skipper."

"Okay. They'll be taking a paid vacation, so you better be thinking about some new help. Never mind—I'll send you some. Who else, Johnny?"

"What?"

"Witnesses. Where're all the broads I usually see around here?"

"I sent them out on the bay, Max. They're skiing."

"Before or after?"

"Uh . . ."

"Before or after, Johnny?"

"After."

The Man sighed. "Nobody's going to get hurt, Johnny. Now, dammit, how many times I have to tell you that?"

The big crew chief lumbered over, smiling soberly. "Okay, we got it. Within a fifty-yard radius, anyway. Heck says it's more'n half a mile from here. Can you beat that? Two head hits and a lateral running pickoff at better'n half a mile?"

"I can't beat it, Too Bad," the Man replied. "Can you?"

"Wish I could. Heck and me are going up to check it out, if that's okay with you."

"Do that," the Man replied. He gave Royal a hurt look and walked off across the patio. Royal followed with his eyes as the boss of Acapulco went on to the pier and engaged the skipper in a brief conversation.

Moments later, the cruiser was roaring away and the Man was walking slowly back toward the house.

So. He was bringing the girls back. Too bad. Too damned bad for them.

Royal went to the bar and filled a tumbler with Scotch.

Max did not rejoin him, but sauntered idly about the patio.

Jorge was already gone.

JR's own security men had been whisked away.

He felt suddenly naked, stripped of all the pretense upon which his life had been built—and John Royal began to see himself in the bottom of the glass of Scotch.

His villa? This was not *his* villa. It belonged to the company—the corporation—the outfit. Everything in it belonged to them. *Just mind the store, Johnny.* Sure. The whore store. The one and only John Royal was nothing more than a whoremaster. A rose, by any other name . . .

Now, even the stiffs were gone, the telltale

bricks scrubbed clean, the "embarrassing" corpses whisked away somewhere to probably never turn up again.

The company took care of its own, sure.

Some day, probably, they'd be taking care of JR himself with that same efficiency. Well, what the hell—it had been a good life, most of the time.

Too Bad and Heck returned, solemnly excited and keeping it cool. They'd found the "drop." Apparently they'd found something else, as well. They showed it to the Man and—for the first time in memory—JR saw Max the Boss lose his cool.

The mighty one did a double take on that "find"—and then he did something really insane. He stormed over and *kicked* the chaise longue on which, minutes earlier, had reposed the remains of Bobby Cassiopea. A symbolic gesture, no doubt.

"*Idiot!*" he screamed. "You fuckin' *idiot!*"

And Johnny Royal knew, in that moment, that something terrible had come to Acapulco, the paradise of the golden gods. Whatever it was, it obviously had come with Cassiopea—and it had killed him—and it had overturned, with three claps of the gavel, the cozy retirement of the one and only John Royal.

The world had changed. JR knew that with certainty, no matter how the thing finally turned.

He lifted his glass to the abused chaise and quietly toasted it. "Here's to change," he said, and meant it.

3: The Scorch

Bolan was in standard uniform for the Acapulco idle—swim trunks, casual shirt, sandals. It provided a comforting anonymity. On the other side of the ledger, it was impossible to properly conceal a weapon in such a get-up. He was not, however, anticipating an immediate need for weaponry.

He was on a soft mission.

He found the lady at her hotel, the Acapulco Royal, sipping coffee in the "island" dining room—a patio restaurant completely surrounded by a moatlike swimming pool. He spotted her from the bridge and recognized her immediately, which was not at all difficult. She was perhaps the most beautiful woman in Mack Bolan's experience. The skin was sun-bronzed while suggesting a texture as soft as rose petals, the hair a shining contrast of softly waved gold framing the unforgettable face—widely spaced deep-set eyes, luscious mouth.

She wore a white see-through bolero jacket which was meant only to enhance, certainly not to conceal, the mind-boggling configuration of planes and angles beneath. The bikini itself was a minor technicality of dress code. In this package, what you saw was truth in advertising. Even in this land of perpetual flesh display, this lady would be a traffic stopper. And, no, there was no problem with the identification.

Bolan pulled out a chair and sat down opposite her. "I have bad news," he said quietly.

Cool blue eyes took his measure before that pleasant voice calmly advised him, "You're in a no-parking zone, *turisto*."

He figured she could handle it. He gave it to her, right between the eyes. "Cass is dead."

Something quivered there, in that cool gaze, but it was the only reaction as she parried that charge. "Well, it *is* a unique approach. I guess now I'm supposed to ask, 'Who is Cass?' And then you'll say—"

"He took a bullet through the head on JR's patio." Bolan could have been discussing the menu, for all the emotion he was putting into it. "Right now I'd guess he's in a weighted bag, somewhere in the cool depths of Pacifico. You see—it was the worst possible time, at the worst possible place. The Man is reacting in typical fashion, scorching every inch of earth between himself and the event. Your time is very short. If this were a parking zone, lady, I wouldn't invest a single *centavo* in your meter."

She was fumbling for a cigarette, obviously trying to cover a rising confusion.

He gave her time to get it together, then held a flame to the cigarette as he told her, "I'm your only way out. Now or never. You stand up right now and walk out of here with me or you're shark bait for sure."

The lady had guts. And she was no dummy. A bit of color had departed that lovely face but it was the only sign of the emotions working at her. The voice remained cool and together. "How do I know you're not one of the sharks?"

"You don't," he replied, and stood up.

She casually scooped up her purse, dropped some coins onto the table, and rose gracefully to join him. Truth in advertising, yeah. With double the effect, standing. Bolan wondered fleetingly what it was like to live inside a body like that, to have the entire world halt and jerk its head at every step you took.

Apparently this one had learned to live with it. Or maybe to enjoy it.

"Beautiful," she murmured. "Your place or mine?"

"Mine," he said curtly, and took her quickly away from there.

Bolan knew the lady well, though this was their first meeting. Her name was Martha Canada. Friends and associates called her Marty. Age twenty-five, career girl but not particularly militant about it, degree in business arts from Michigan State. Daddy was a retired GM executive. Mother deceased. Brother Jeremy a third-year student at Ohio State.

She'd been with Cassiopea for only about a year, having dropped out of a post-grad course at Pontiac to accept the employment offer. Cass, Baby had picked her out of a lineup of beauty contestants at the Michigan State Fair—but apparently he had tailored the job offer to fit her academic qualifications—which, in all fairness, were very good. She was a showpiece, though—Bolan was certain of that. Officially she'd been the guy's executive secretary—a *traveling* secretary. A dream job, under most any other circumstances. Constant travel to all the major world capitals, continual contact with the beautiful and powerful people everywhere—all expenses paid, and a handsome salary to boot.

Yeah. Bolan's file on Martha Canada was detailed and complete, but still he did not know the inner secrets of this lady. And he did not know the full depth of her association with the mob's glamour boy of international finance.

The drive to his bungalow at Las Brisas—the fabulous hotel in the hills above the east bay—was a short and silent run. He made no attempt at conversation, nor did she. Apparently she'd known where they were headed from the moment she stepped into the jeep. The pink and white vehicles were a sort of trademark of Las Brisas—a special service to their guests.

She broke the silence when he wheeled onto the terraced grounds of the hotel complex, though it

27

was a bit of an absent-minded query—spoken from a corner of her consciousness. "Are there really two hundred swimming pools?"

Bolan shrugged and fielded the question on the same level as given. "I haven't had time to count them. Anyway, they're sort of small."

"It all looks very nice," she said quietly.

Nice, yeah. Two hundred and fifty bungalows, or *casitas*, each with its own stocked bar and private pool, each nestled onto its own terrace behind flowering hedges to insure total privacy. Nice for honeymooners, or house nudists, or for celebrities seeking anonymity in a quiet, private club atmosphere. The accommodations were swank and the service impeccable. An American travel writer had recently hailed Las Brisas as one of the three finest hotels in the world. Bolan could believe it. And the seclusion was doubly nice for a guy in his situation.

The lady was telling him, "I had hoped that we would stay here this time. Mr. Cassiopea prefers the show and tell crowd, though."

Naturally. "Show and tell" was Cass Baby's chief stock in trade.

Bolan helped her out of the jeep and guided her along the path to his *casita*. She paused just outside, sighing—perhaps appreciating the breathtaking view of Acapulco Bay, perhaps trying to collect her mind and come to some final decision regarding the stranger beside her and that ultraprivate bungalow to which he was escorting her.

"It's okay," he gruffly told her. "You have nothing to fear from me."

"Why did you bring me here?"

"You don't have to stay," he told her. "Follow the path on around to the office. You can get a cab from there."

"What's it like inside?" she asked, peering at the *casita*.

He opened the door and stood aside. "Check it out if you'd like," he offered.

She showed him a wobbly smile and went inside. "Oh, it's quite nice," she called from the interior.

Bolan went in and closed the door. "Bar's over there," he said, pointing. "If you don't see what you like, call the desk."

She helped herself from the fruit bowl, instead, and dropped onto a longue near the window, clutching a *zapote* rather absently in both hands.

In here, suddenly, it was all very different. Mack Bolan was a man of singular purpose, indeed, and he had little time or energies for a pursuit of the mating game. He was not, however, immune to the tug of masculine sensibilities—and this lady was something very special. The place was, too; together, yeah, it was suddenly all very different. She was very appealing, distracting, troubling.

He lit a cigarette and turned his gaze onto the bay. "It is beautiful, isn't it," he small-talked.

"Oh, very." She seemed as uncomfortable as he.

"I suppose you're wondering what I'm about."

29

"I'm working at it," she quietly admitted. "You're obviously not Mexican police. So what does that make you? FBI? CIA? What?"

"Friend," he replied quietly. "If you can accept that."

She shook her head. "That isn't enough. You've probably made the whole thing up." She was kidding while not kidding, ticking off the possibilities, seeking sanity in an insane situation, voicing it all in the same frame of mind as a whistler in the dark. "Either I've been kidnapped—or Cass is going to walk through that door any minute and we're all going to be laughing over a very brutal practical joke, or—"

He had to shut that off. "Call him, then."

She looked surprised and relieved, all at once. "Call Cass?"

"Give it a try, yeah."

"Where do I reach him?"

"I've already told you that. To satisfy your doubts, though, give it a try. Try JR."

"Try who?"

"JR."

"Why should I call JR? I don't even know JR."

"You're Cass Baby's secretary. There must be a couple of reasons why you need to contact him. Call the actor."

She again shook that lovely head at him. "No I—I'm not supposed to even *know* about JR."

"But you do."

Her color changed ever so slightly. "Yes. I do."

"How *much* do you know?"

Those eyes blinked rapidly. "This is beginning to sound like a third degree. Let's go back to just being friends."

He said it flatly. "You knew about Cass's mob connections."

Her gaze settled on the fruit in her lap. "I've suspected," she admitted. "Nothing that I could really pin down. But, well, you can't travel the world with someone for a year and not notice peculiar little things. Yes, I've wondered about him. Believe it or not, I had decided to make this my final trip. I was going to give him notice when we got back to Detroit."

"Could it be that simple?"

"What do you mean?"

"There were no personal complications between you?"

She smiled wryly at the *zapote* and gave a rather bitter little reply to that accusation. "My own father thinks the same way."

"It's a natural assumption," Bolan said lightly. "Most of the world thinks that way."

"Well, think again," she said. "Is he really dead?"

Bolan nodded his head. "Does the thought tear you up?"

"Later, maybe. Right now I'm just sort of numb. But listen, I—why should I care what *you* think? Who *are* you?"

He smiled and said, "Later. First, I need a perspective on your relationship to the deceased."

"Strictly business," she muttered. "I respected

him, I liked him—at first—but there was absolutely nothing else between us." She lifted those great eyes to search his. "Is he really dead?"

Bolan sighed and handed her the telephone. "Call your hotel. Ask for Cassiopea. But don't identify yourself."

"What will that prove, if he isn't there?"

Bolan said, "Just do it. If I've read the Man correctly, you could be in for a revealing surprise."

"Who is this *man* you keep talking about?"

"Just do it. Make the call, dammit."

She did, and her gaze lurched at Bolan as she replied to some information from her hotel switchboard. "Of course he's registered," she said angrily.

"Find out if *you* are," Bolan suggested.

Her eyes flashed. "Let me speak to Miss Canada, then—Miss Martha Canada."

Bolan muttered, "Get ready for a shock."

She whispered, "Thank you," into the telephone, hung up, and said to Bolan, "Well, that is very weird. They say that neither of us is registered there."

"The Man works very fast his wonders to perform," Bolan soberly told her. "You want to know who he is? He's the sultan of Acapulco and points south. He runs a very tight ship, and right now, I'm afraid, Martha Canada is a glaringly loose end in his scorched earth cover-up. Are you convinced?"

The girl bit her lip as she dug into the purse

for a small memo book. She riffled the pages, found the information she sought, and again worked the telephone.

"Play it cool," Bolan advised. "Tell nobody where you are."

Her eyes signaled that understanding and remained fixed on Bolan's cold gaze while she awaited the connection.

"Yes, *buenas tardes*—do you speak English?"

That wide-eyed gaze maintained penetrating contact with Bolan.

"Yes, thank you. I am Martha Canada. I am Mr. Cassiopea's secretary. I was told I could reach him at this number. Yes, thank you."

She covered the transmitter and reported to Bolan, "It's a man with a Mexican accent. He's gone to ask someone."

"Oh, yes—who is this again, please? John *Royal*! Oh. I'm sorry to disturb you—I didn't know. Mr. Cassiopea left this number in case of—is he there?"

She signaled Bolan with her fingers and angled the receiver outward for his monitoring. He leaned forward, his face touching hers, to listen to a very familiar voice.

"... and don't ask any questions, Miss, just listen and take it for gospel. Don't go to your hotel—don't go *near* it. They're probably waiting for you there. Don't ask who *they* are and don't doubt for a minute that there's nothing left for you in this town, so do as I say. Don't go to the cops, and for God's sake not to the American consulate. Just get out of the country as fast as you can shake it."

"Mr. Royal, I—"

"Wait, better not try the airport. They could be looking for you there, too. Take a bus to Mexico City and work out something from there. If it was me, lady, I'd hire a cab to Mexico City. Listen, don't call here again and don't—"

"Mr. Royal! Where *is* Mr. Cassiopea?"

"Don't you have it yet, lady? I never heard of the guy—and, if you're smart, neither did you."

Royal hung up.

Bolan took the phone from a dazed young lady as he told her, "The town is shaking with scorched earth."

"But why?" she whispered. "It's *crazy.*"

He pressed a marksman's medal into her hand. "Because of this," he said quietly. "And because of the Acapulco Conference."

"What is this?" she asked, inspecting the bull's-eye cross with troubled eyes.

"It's my signature," he told her. "My name is Bolan."

"Far out!" she gasped, and fainted dead away.

He lifted that technically nude body in gentle arms and carried her to the bed. His hands tingled from the touch of her, and transmitted shock waves in reverberating patterns from his skull to his feet.

"You're quite a scorcher, yourself," he told the unconscious beauty, then went to the bathroom to wet a towel.

No, dammit, it was no time for fun and games, love and laughter.

The Executioner had come to Acapulco for an all-consuming purpose.

He had come to shake their Mexican house down.

4: The Smell

Acapulco is one of those rare constellations of the North American scene, a truly international resort city. It is Las Vegas set to water, minus the casinos—Miami Beach shrunk to country club size to combine free spirit with clannish intimacy—Cannes without a film festival.

And more, of course. Acapulco is perpetual Carnival with elbow room—in two parts. Part One is sunshine, sand, and water—sightseeing and deep sea fishing, waterskis and parachute rides over the bay, shopping and munching or just people-watching at the *zocalo*—and the standard costume is bikini and/or beach togs, with the accent always on ease and comfort.

Part Two is welcome siesta and colorful sunsets, gourmet dining under the stars and/or in swank surroundings, cocktails in bunches and spectacular entertainment—house parties, yacht parties, beach parties, discotheques, stripjoints, wherever the mood or opportunity inclines—and the dress here is theatrical bordering on the bizarre. Part Two *chic* for the ladies indulges and encourages their fondest fantasies. As one noted observer has stated, the selection of evening attire is not so much a question of what to wear as who to be. From hot pants to gypsy skirts, sequined slacks to denim jeans, kaftans to braless peek-a-boo—the look is entirely up to the lady, limited only by imagination and courage.

For the men, the costume is comfort. Ties and stiff collars are an unspoken taboo. Comfortable slacks, soft shoes, and fancy shirts are prevalent, with here and there a billowing smock or belted kaftan, a shoulder bag, even a headband and, more and more, free-swinging lockets or charms around the neck on sturdy chains.

Carnival, yeah, but not the hysterical flesh traps of Rio or New Orleans. The Carnival of Acapulco is a perpetual life-style (for the fortunate ones), and it is a thing primarily of the spirit.

There are, also, two Acapulcos. One hovers at the water line or perches on spectacular overlooks, rising high into the azure sky or sprawling along terraced hillsides. The other packs itself onto the narrow strip of earth between the bay and the steep mountains rising to encircle it, and it is here that the quarter-million or so natives live their lives and conduct their daily affairs.

The bay is semicircular—formed, actually, by a pair of peninsulas jutting generally southward into the Pacific in a sort of pincers movement.

The west peninsula is "old town," the original settlement. Near its base is situated the *zocalo*, or town square, and the principal business district. The older and cheaper hotels are here, as is most of the color and the old world charm of this very colorful city. Towards the southern end of this peninsula are the bullring and *jai alai* amphitheater, the "morning beaches," beautiful Roqueta Island.

At the top of old town, on the Pacific side, soars famed La Quebrada, the cliff from which daredevil divers perform for the tourists.

On the bay side are the yacht club, Honda and Manzanillo Beaches, then circling northeasterly to the top of the bay and Hornos, the "afternoon beach," La Condesa Beach—the swingers' haven (gays to the east, please), and the beginning of high-rise luxury hotels.

Bolan's hotel occupied a hillside overlooking the bay from the east peninsula. Southward from there lay the little companion bay, Puerto Marques, and its Pichelingue Beach, site of the plush villas of the Acapulco elite. On the Pacific side, south, is Revolcadero Beach and its impressive great pyramid hotel, the Princess.

Bolan had selected Las Brisas not only for the relative seclusion and privacy but also because of its geographic place. The east bay was the haunt of the international jet set, and it was here that Bolan's business was. Movie and TV personalities as well as various world celebrities were as common here as stars in a cloudless night. It was in this atmosphere of glamour and wealth that the new Mafia was establishing franchises and founding empires. It was here that the New Mafia, *La Nuova Cosa Nostra*, was being forged.

The Acapulco Conference was not so much an event as a continually revolving door, through which big time hoods or their emissaries from throughout the world scurried to make bids and seal deals which would guarantee their places in the new empire.

Max Spielke—known variously as the Sultan, the Man, and *Capo Mexicano*—was hosting the affair. That latter "title" was an honorary one. Spielke was Jewish, not Italian. He was nevertheless the boss of underground Mexico, and all knew it, the Italians as well as the others.

Acapulco had obviously been regarded as an ideal setting for this new approach to criminal congress, successor to the aborted and disastrous Montreal Meet which had herded them all together in one time and place, ripe for the pickings by an audacious interloper like Mack the Bastard Bolan. Acapulco was a back door to the continent, and it was a constantly swinging one, admitting without fanfare the great and illustrious of the world as well as their antitypes.

Bolan himself had experienced no difficulty whatever in entering the country. He'd picked up a tourist card along with his plane ticket at the airline office in the U.S. Personal identification was never a problem. It was easily and cheaply available almost anywhere—birth certificate, passport, driver's license, credit cards; if it could be printed or manufactured, it could be bought.

Probably none of those attending the Acapulco Conference were required to worry about such matters, however. They were not fugitives, like Bolan. Even if their movements were being watched by various governments, there would be nothing particularly ominous or even suspicious about a brief vacation to the golden city.

There were other favorable conditions, as well. The official tenor of the Mexican government had recently been toward a leadership role in the Third World of developing nations. Diplomatic and business channels had been widening rapidly in directions pointedly away from the American continent—and a whole new playground was emerging for the Mafia money men who were constantly alert to new and better laundry facilities for their black bucks.

Also, official Mexico had long been the golden land of *mordida*—the payoff, the kickback. Officials on the take were a rule rather than an exception, and no one seemed to expect them to behave much differently. The *mafiosi* must have felt right at home in such an environment. Certainly they would know how to exploit the situation to the best possible results.

Bolan and the Canadian cops had shown them in Montreal the folly of mobbing up in an open convention atmosphere. So this time they were trying Acapulco and a revolving door conference, stealthy meetings in small groups, using the beautiful people themselves as their covers.

But Mack Bolan had been with them all the way. Very little of importance happened in the world of Mafia without his knowledge. He was known primarily by his thundering effect, but intelligence was his really strong suit. Without it, there could be no thunder. It was as much a defensive as an offensive weapon; without it, he would have perished long ago.

He'd been onto Cassiopea, of course, since before the Detroit death watch and the first faint rumbles of Montreal—even while the federal strike forces were still whispering the guy's code name.

Spielke was not that familiar an item. The Mexican arm of the mob had until very recently functioned mostly as a sort of vacation Mafia, almost as a consular function administered for the benefit of vacationing or low-lying hoods. The Man was the one with the contacts, the *mordida* master and jet-set manipulator. Bolan had rarely heard the guy's name in any other context. He owned a huge yacht, one of the most impressive villas in the area, and was generally regarded as among the wealthiest and most influential men on the Mexican Pacific coast.

Acapulco was his turf, though, and all who ventured there were warned of the fact. Nothing moved through that underworld area without paying a tax to the Man, none entered without his prior consent, no "business" was transacted except at his pleasure. So it was a tight area—and a quiet one, mob-wise. Bolan's jungle telegraph had brought him very little news of Mexico, until very recently. Suddenly Acapulco appeared as a major port for heroin and cocaine movements. Then there were rumbles about the international traffic in top-grade party girls, with Acapulco centering as the route of entry into the jet set and all that implied.

Finally, via a watchful eye on Cass Baby, Bolan got wind of *La Nuova Cosa Nostra* and the Acapulco Conference. He'd been watching them at close range for more than a week now, and this first rumble of thunder was no more than the opening gun of a meticulously planned war.

As to just how deeply involved in all this was the stunning young woman now lying rather nakedly upon his bed, Bolan could not even hazard a guess. He definitely had mixed feelings about the lady, not the least of which were centered upon his own responses to her.

He had approached her with two minds—one very genuinely concerned about her safety, the other curious about the "girlie" angle of the Acapulco scene and wondering whether Martha Canada might shed a bit of light in that dark corner. Logic told him that the lady could not travel with wolves and not carry their odor. And yet . . .

She was stirring and beginning to fight the cold towel. He tossed it aside and asked her, "Okay now?"

Her eyes recoiled from his close gaze. "What—what happened?" she inquired in a choked voice.

He showed her half a smile. "An accumulation of things, I guess. You passed out on me."

Awareness abruptly returned, then, and the lady was not enjoying any of it. Her gaze bounced around the room as she asked him, "Why did you bring me here?"

"Not what you're thinking, I'll bet," he assured her. "You're here, Marty, because I couldn't think of another safe port for you. You know who I am, don't you."

"I know *what* you are," she said dully. "The name was loud and clear."

If you want honesty, you catch them at the borderline of consciousness. The lady did not take to the likes of a Mack Bolan. He accepted that judgment without a flicker of protest, and consigned it to his mental file.

"Then you probably understand that I'm the one who hit Cass Baby. I also took out his companions of the moment—the drug king of Central America and his Honduran lieutenant. They were having a parley on JR's patio, setting up some new distribution routes, no doubt, for the Kingdom of Misery. But that's not all; it's just the beginning."

"The beginning of what?" she muttered.

"The new world. It's a Mafia world, lady, and they intend to carve it up right here in Acapulco. They have a lot of tools, and they're going to work on the weaknesses of the old world. That translates to sex, drugs, greed, the lusting for power, simple egomania, fear, poverty, resignation. You name it, they know all the symptoms and they know just where to make the cut."

She whispered, "You've been seeing too many *macho* movies."

"Baloney," he replied mildly. "Hollywood doesn't have the guts, the understanding, or the ability to tell it like it really is down here in the slime pits. I've been living here for a long time. Where've you been living?"

She twitched at that, and turned her face to the wall.

Bolan bored on. "Cass's chief preoccupation for the past few months has been with the flesh lines. He's been introducing into the new world a steady stream of attractive young ladies with ready bottoms, willing eyes, and charm school manners—entirely captivating young ladies who can be very nice to tired old political hacks, over-the-hill generals, and anyone in need with something to trade. That's just the one side of it. The other side involves extortion, blackmail, grand larceny on a cosmic scale, treason. On which side did you fit, Marty?"

"Go to hell," the girl muttered.

"And then of course there's an occasional murder or minor atrocity—a torture-slaying here and there—a young girl who couldn't quite hack it on the flesh lines sent to oblivion in the slave markets."

44

She was slowly coming off the wall. "You don't really believe all that stuff."

"I have to believe it. I've seen it."

"From what I hear, you've *done* it," she snapped.

He shrugged. "I've never killed a civilized man. And I've never misused a woman, of any type. Not yet."

"That's a threat, isn't it."

"It's just a fact," he replied, showing her some teeth.

Bolan left the bed and went to the closet for his clothing. He started his packing, and told the girl: "I'll be leaving. The soft watch is over and I'll be going to my hard base. The rent is paid up here through the end of the week. Stay, if you'd like. I suggest that you do."

She was sitting up, now, giving him the curious eye. "That's it?"

"It is," he said. "Take care. I hope you get back home in one piece."

"You really think I'm in danger?"

"You heard the king of the silver screen, didn't you? Of course you're in danger. The Man is on a panic run. Too much is at stake here to have it toppled by a mere killing or two."

"I guess I just don't understand the logic."

Bolan went on with his packing as he explained the logic to the lady. "If I'm walking along the street out here and two cars come together, and one of the cars catches fire, and I dash over and pull the victims from the burning car, and they're already dead—do you know what's going to happen to me?"

She was looking at him very strangely, now. "Well, you're a wanted man. You couldn't risk—"

"Before that, even, before I was identified—the chances are very strong that I would be summarily hauled off to jail, tossed into a rat-infested black hole, and rot there until all the facts were known and all blame finally established regarding the deaths of the victims. I'm no hero, see—I'm guilty of what the Mexicans call *mal medicina*. I moved an injured person, and the person died—or maybe they were already dead when I moved them. The point is that they observe the Napoleonic Code in Mexico. I'm guilty until proven innocent—and that usually takes a hell of a long time. Meanwhile, sure, my sordid past surfaces to bite me, and I'll probably never see the outside world again."

"So?" she asked, interest rising.

"Well, so, Max the Man has a lot of clout around here—and I doubt very much that he would be unduly affected by a murder in his own bedroom. But even a half-hearted investigation into that guy's closets would release more skeletons than all the clout in Mexico could cover up. And the timing is so bad, see. There's this world-carving conference I told you about. No, the Man doesn't want any real trouble with the authorities here—not even if he owns half of them. The more they have on him, the deeper their hands reach into his pockets. He has to cover himself, protect the conference, erase any possible link between himself and the victims. But he probably wouldn't kill you, Marty."

"Why do you say that?"

"He'd sell you."

"What?"

"Or maybe he'd just give you away. To a desert sheik, maybe, who's earned a favor. Or to an African chief with friendly influence in a developing market. Or maybe to a whoremaster in Algiers, as a special bonus."

The girl had turned positively ashen. Very quietly, she asked him, "Are you serious?"

"I never make sick jokes," he assured her.

She blew then.

"For God's sake, don't leave me here alone!"

"I'm afraid I have no choice, Marty."

"But he'll find me. You don't know—I *do*! Max is like *God* around here! If he wants me, he'll *find* me!"

Yeah. Sure. If you want honesty, you catch them at the borderline of consciousness—or at the edge of panic.

Honesty, sometimes, can be very painful. For a man with uncertain emotions, especially so.

A very pained Mack Bolan told the lady, "Okay, Marty. You're probably not worth it ... but I'll take you with me."

Sure. She had their smell on her.

5: The Hook

Shops and stores along the way were opening their doors; the town was coming alive again; *siesta* was over. There was plenty of action along the beaches and on the bay, though, since visitors generally took their *siesta* at sundown.

Bolan had changed into bell-bottom white ducks, deck shoes, nautical shirt and skipper's hat. He wore, also, a .38 chief's special in snap-rig strapped to the inside of his left leg, concealed beneath the belled pants leg.

He stopped at one of the shops and picked up a cotton beach wrap for the lady, also a sun hat to cover that golden head. She accepted the gifts without comment and put them on.

Bolan then drove directly to the marina. He transferred the girl and his gear to the power boat he'd rented shortly after his arrival in the resort city, then took the jeep back to the parking area and left it there.

The attendant had been watching him through

the window all the while. Bolan stepped inside the office to lay a few pesos on the guy.

The attendant pocketed the money with the standard smile. "I see you have company this time, *Señor* Franklin. Will you require skis?"

"*Gracias*, no," Bolan replied.

The smile broadened. "Fishing, maybe?"

"Maybe," Bolan said, and returned to the pier.

Marty was seated tensely in the front seat. It was a sixteen-foot inboard/outboard with plenty of poop and comfortable appointments. The girl had removed her hat and wrap.

Bolan frowned at that as he moved in beside her. He kicked the engine and got up to cast off.

"I can do that," Marty offered.

"Stay put," he growled. "And put your hat on."

The attendant was watching them through binoculars.

"Is something wrong?" the girl asked Bolan, reading his face probably more than his growl.

"Maybe." He cast off the lines and moved away at a sedate idling speed. "Can you handle a boat?" he asked her.

"Sure."

He turned it over to her with the simple instruction, "Head south." Then he broke out his own binoculars.

The guy was still watching them. And he now had a telephone to his ear.

It was not much, but enough to put the Bolan combat senses on edge. He went aft to his gear and made ready his weapons. When he returned to take over the wheel, the gleaming AutoMag .44 was strapped to his hip in open leather and a wicked little Uzi submachine gun dangled from a shoulder strap.

They were well clear of the marina now, but Bolan was still casting his attention that way.

Marty took note of the weaponry with obvious distaste. "What are you doing?" she asked, in a frightened voice.

"Staying alive, maybe," he told her. He stowed the Uzi underfoot then took the wheel and immediately swung it hard a'port, accelerating into a wide power turn and heading toward the east side of the bay.

The girl lost her hat and shivered slightly under the sudden spray.

"You okay?" he asked her, in a softer tone.

"Sure," she said, and left it there.

Neither had found much to say to the other since the departure from Las Brisas. The mood between them had been one of almost brooding restraint. Once, during the drive to the marina, she had timidly ventured a sort of half-apology. "I guess I'm putting you in some sort of double joepardy."

"We'll see," was his only response to that.

But, sure, the truth of the matter was that Martha Canada's presence at his side posed a definite hazard and heavy liability to Bolan's Acapulco effort.

Bolan himself was a sort of ghost. He was there but not there, visible but hardly recognizable since few living enemies had ever seen his face or even a respectable likeness of it. They knew him by image and reputation only, and he took pains to keep it that way.

Also, Bolan moved with care and watched his tracks, ever alert and responsive to enemy presence, and he was always ready to meet the enemy head-on or to stand down quickly in graceful retreat, if that seemed advisable. For every path forward, he usually managed to engineer several alternatives including one or two to the rear.

So, yes, the lady was definitely a problem. The enemy *knew* her, and they probably had eyes everywhere looking for her. A light such as that was pretty hard to hide under a bushel. The guy at the marina had certainly noted it, and the chances were excellent that he'd reported the sighting into the Man's telegraph system.

She was going to mess him up, for damn sure.

But what the hell could he *do* with her?

He could, he knew with a resignation born of many such situations, do only as he was doing. Drag her along, and hope for the best. With a few necessary changes to his own plan of attack. Yeah. It was the only way. He could not change her place in the general run of things—but he *could*, maybe, change her relative importance.

He could give the Man something else to think about. Something, maybe, that would make him forget for a while that the lady even existed.

And this was the present thrust.

"That's Max's yacht!" the girl cried, pointing to a sleek craft looming up on their starboard bow.

"That's what it is," Bolan agreed.

"You aren't taking me *there*?"

"Either you trust me or you don't," he replied, yelling to make himself heard above the roar of the motor. "If you don't, it's time to get off."

"Thanks, I'll stay," she yelled back.

The big yacht was riding anchor off Guitarron Beach, at the south end of the bay. Fully fifty to sixty feet long and deep drafted for transoceanic service, she was designed to be propelled by sails or power, or both in combination, and she was a thing to delight the nautical heart.

Any Acapulco regular could tell the curious tourist about the *Seaward,* with her fabulous salon where thirty people could sit down and eat together—or get drunk and raise hell together— or go to bed together in her many plush cabins, with fine appointments to satisfy the most luxury-loving landlubber.

It was said that Spielke loved nothing in all the world more than he loved that boat. To be invited aboard was a singular honor. To be a guest at one of the rare parties in her salon was a social triumph. To be included on a cruise to Puerto Vallarta or some other nearby port meant that you had made the blue book of international society.

Bolan knew from his own close investigation that the Man studiously avoided any cross-relation between his beloved yacht and his "business" life. He never held meetings there. He did not entertain visiting hoods there. Most of the time, it was said, the boat just sat there, riding anchor, with a two-man caretaker crew who saw to the security and kept everything shipshape. When Spielke used her for entertaining, he brought people from his household staff to mind the chores. For the infrequent voyages, he hired local sailors to round out the crew for proper ship-handling.

Right now she was just sitting there, riding anchor off Guitarron Beach. Spielke's villa was on a coastal bluff overlooking the anchorage; it gave him pleasure just to look out and see her riding there. He did have a deep-water pier immediately below the house, with direct access via stairway, but the *Seaward* was too much boat—and perhaps a bit too deep-drafted—for accommodation there.

Bolan cut his power at fifty yards out and asked the lady, "Have you been aboard?"

"No," she replied quietly.

"Ever invited aboard?"

"Never."

"Would you like to go aboard?"

She shivered. "No way."

"Fine, because I have other things in mind for you."

She shivered again, this one much more pronounced. "What are we doing?"

"We're hijacking a beloved yacht."

"What?"

"Yeah. Dirty trick, isn't it." He was studying the *Seaward*, trying to read her inner secrets. A big-chested guy in dungarees and white shirt was on the flying bridge, staring back at him. Another was on the main deck forward, fooling with the rigging. "Looks easy from here. I'm going aboard, Marty. Soon as I do, circle off—but stay close—within swimming distance."

"I just hope you know what you're doing," she commented miserably.

He chuckled and told her, "So do I."

A moment later, they were alongside and Bolan was moving onto the gangway. A dinghy was tied there. He cast it loose and sent it skimming along in Marty's wake.

The guy on the bridge yelled something and came quickly down the ladder. Bolan met him at the quarterdeck and showed him the snout of the AutoMag.

And, yeah, it was easy.

True to Bolan's guess, there were no gunners on board. The crewmen were *mestizos*—Mexican nationals of Spanish-Indian stock—and neither exhibited any desire to challenge the authority of Bolan's big blaster.

"Are you the skipper?" Bolan asked Bigchest.

The guy was looking at the gun, not at the man behind it. "*Si.* I am the skipper."

"We're getting underway. Get to it."

The crewmen exchanged unhappy glances, then silently got to it. They stowed the gangway, fired the engines, raised the anchor.

Marty was lying off to the rear, at about a hundred feet.

Bolan went to the flying bridge and looked over the layout there.

"Where do we go, señor?" asked Bigchest.

"Not *we*," Bolan corrected him. He tossed a lifejacket at the guy. "Goodbye," he said. "Take the other guy with you."

There was no mistaking the meaning of that. Bigchest seemed very happy with the order. He shouted something at the other man as he quickly descended to the main deck, and both were over the side in a twinkling.

Bolan watched as they stroked for the dinghy, then he dismissed them from his mind and turned his attention to the *Seaward*.

It *was* a hell of a ship.

He had to squelch a rising tide of regret over his plans for her as he meshed the big power plant and the sleek craft smoothly responded to quarter speed forward. She was not built for speed—eight to ten knots in standard cruising, probably—but she handled like a dream, smooth and quick to the command. And, yeah, Bolan hated to do it to her.

He did it, though.

He brought her around and set her course, locked in the auto-pilot, and sent the engines to full speed forward. After a moment to confirm the true path ahead, he then went below and dived over the side.

Marty picked him up almost as soon as he broke surface.

"What are you doing?" she cried. "There's nobody left on there. And it's—"

Bolan growled, "Yeah. Damned shame, isn't it."

He was sending *Seaward* home.

Home to Max, who loved her so.

At full speed forward, and no one aboard.

6: The Crunch

Spielke's palatial hillside villa, near the entrance to Acapulco Bay, had quickly become something of a fortress.

Two Indians in a jeep, casually watching the front drive, did not challenge Royal's vehicle— but they had a radio, and he knew that they were passing the word inside.

It was a different story, at the gate to the compound. The guys there went over that car like border customs men. One guy even patted Royal down for a weapon—and they did not clear the vehicle for entry until positive that it was virgin pure.

Inside was an armed camp. Indians and *mestizos* were everywhere, patrolling in pairs and armed to the teeth—here and there a *criollo* (a Mexican of pure European heritage) in an Australian bush hat—the mark of rank in this tightly disciplined force.

It was the Sultan's private army, occasionally

whispered about in certain quarters but rarely visible. The only other time Royal had actually seen this force was during the state visit by Augie Marinello and the New York combine of bosses. Rumor had it that they were customarily quartered down on the Costa Chica, near the Oaxaca border—the Afro-Mexican veldt. The force supposedly numbered some two hundred men, including the officers—and had a village of their own where they lived with wives and children. The fact that they were now deployed at Acapulco lent emphasis to the gravity of the situation there.

Royal found himself again scrutinized and detained at the parking area. One of Too Bad's boys had to come down from the house to identify him and escort him inside.

It was some kind of far-out joint. The architecture was what Royal termed *Mediterranean Bastard*. The basic construction was of cement block with fake adobe plastered over the outside and painted a soothing pink. There were also tons of cantilevered steel and special engineering marvels to allow the mass to be hung on the mountainside in just that fashion.

A tri-level job with a full acre under roof, on every level the entire ocean side had walls of glass. The floors were tiered, so that each of the many bedrooms on the upper levels had their own private patio garden. The main level boasted a huge semicircular garden area, complete with fountains and the works, projecting out over the sea. This was fantasyland, even for the jaded jet set. There was a full "bar under the stars" with a dozen stools and a hardwood dance floor. There were umbrella tables, set up like a sidewalk café and attended with the most gracious of continental service. There was a swimming pool, with glass panels open to the sea so that one could dive into its depths for a fish-eye view of Acapulco Bay from on high. Finally there were a putting green and two shuffleboard courts.

At the moment, fantasyland had been converted to an emergency command center.

Spielke and his legbreakers sat at a large oval table near the pool. Long extension cords provided individual telephone service for each man at the table—and there were ten of them.

Too Bad Paul sat at the opposite side of the oval from the Man. He was gazing forlornly onto the pages of an international hotel guide, spread open before him.

"This is awful," the crew boss declared as Royal got within earshot. "Did you realize there's thirty-five pages of listings, just for Acapulco?"

"You take them one page at a time, Paul," Spielke growled. "Tear them out and pass them around."

"It's over two hundred damned hotels, sir."

"I don't care if it's two thousand. The guy is here and we have to find him. Or would you prefer that we just call everything off, sit tight, and wait for him to find us?"

"Shouldn't be all that hard," volunteered another lieutenant. "I'll make ten to one the guy travels alone. That narrows the field a hell of a lot. We ask for American males registered as singles. We get that list and start—"

"What if he rented an apartment?" Too Bad growled.

Spielke blinked at that, then replied, "Call that Playasol office. They handle most of the condominiums around here."

"See, it's getting broader as we go along," Too Bad complained.

"Then we'd better get started quick, hadn't we," Spielke retorted acidly.

The crew boss sighed loudly and began tearing out the pages.

Royal's arrival had gone apparently unnoticed. He tried a laugh that failed and said, "Put walls around this table, Max, and you've got a Chicago bookie joint."

The Man did not think that funny. "We're busy as hell, Johnny. What do you want?"

"I was wondering about my girls."

"What about them?"

"What'd you do with them, Max?"

Too Bad snickered.

Spielke glared at the actor for a quiet moment before replying, "I sent them to Tampico."

Royal groaned. "Those are top-quality girls, Max."

"They're a penny a dozen and you know it," the Man replied heavily. "Get out of here, Johnny. Go home and stay put."

"It's scarey there, Max. You said you were sending me a couple of boys to replace Juan and Enrico."

"I changed my mind," Spielke grunted. "Waste of manpower, Johnny. If the guy had wanted you, he would have taken you with Cass and the others. Just go home and sit tight."

Royal steeled himself to say: "Well that's, uh, what I really came to tell you, Max. There's no sense in me hanging around here, with all this going on. You can't use my place until it's cleared up, that's for sure. I got space on the eight o'clock flight to L.A. I figured I—"

"You figured wrong," the Man told him. "I canceled that space twenty minutes ago, Johnny. Don't try it again."

Royal's anger at that news exceeded his common sense. "I come and go as I damn please, Max!" he yelled. "You don't tell me when I come and go!"

A stillness as taut as a drawn bowstring descended upon that gathering. Royal's face remained set in angry lines, but he knew he'd overstepped his line of grace. He lit a cigarette, the lighter clicking overly loud in the pall of silence, and muttered, "I'm sorry, Max. I just don't feel up to it. Gladhanding and bundling a few of your business friends is one thing. Cold-blooded murder and open warfare is something else. I never dealt myself in for anything like this."

A telephone at the table rang. Spielke's gaze

traveled there, then he nodded to the legbreaker closest to it.

Royal gratefully loosened under the welcome interruption and sucked on his cigarette as the guy scooped up the phone and growled into it, "*Por que?*"

"It's Tony," the torpedo reported to the boss. "He says the guy at marina del mar thinks he spotted the Canada chick. She left in a runabout with a guy named Franklin. Says they headed out south, just a few minutes ago."

"Tell Tony to put the helicopter on it, check it out. If it is her, I want her—however they have to get her here."

The legbreaker relayed the message and hung up.

The deadening silence returned.

Spielke began drumming his fingers on the table.

The men at the table were giving Royal silently amused attention.

What the hell? He'd already blown it. May as well go down for doubles. He nervously cleared his throat and said, "Leave the woman alone, Max. She couldn't know a damn thing. You've already buried the bodies and erased every footprint around them. What the hell do you want, for God's sake—holy sacrament?"

The fingers abruptly ceased their drumming.

The other shoe was about to come down.

Very quietly, the man said, "You're a shitbag, do you know that? Who says you dealt yourself into anything? You Hollywood people are all one and the same. Shitbags, and nothing else. If it wasn't for your agents and your managers and all the other shit moulders, you'd still be resting quietly at the bottom of the cesspools where you all started. You've got no head, no belly, and no legs to stand on. Men and women alike, you're all the same. Who ever told you a pearly smile or a wiggling ass made you something special? They write the words for you on a cardboard and you learn how to read them off—and that makes you a special creation, eh?

"I sent for you, kid—you didn't send for me. And you came running for the same reason all the others do. You came because you've got no head, no belly, and no legs—and there's just no other place for a shitbag, is there, after they've torn the shithouse down. Who the hell ever told you that you dealt yourself into something? You *oozed* here, Mr. Hollywood. Now, dammit, let's get something straight, once and for all. You go when and where I tell you to go. You come when and where I tell you to come. And you just sit there and quiver like a nice shitbag when I tell you to do that, too. Do we understand each other, Johnny?"

"Sure," Royal replied quietly, thoroughly crunched. "I told you I was sorry, Max."

Someone at the table chuckled.

The Man said, "Shut up and get to work, you guys."

Royal strolled to the brick parapet, hoping perhaps to find himself—or what was left of himself—in the ocean view.

The Man called to him. Johnny turned back with a forced smile and said, "Here, Max."

"If it will make you feel better, you've got time to kiss those girls goodbye," Spielke softly suggested. "They're leaving at six on the company plane, the Tampico shuttle. Meanwhile I'm wining and dining them at Tres Vidas. Come to think about it, maybe you *should* go. A couple of *amici* are arriving on that plane. You can be the official reception committee."

"Fine," JR replied smoothly. "I'll do that."

"There's plenty of time. Have a drink before you go."

Royal nodded his head agreeably and turned quickly back to the parapet. He could hold that painful smile for just so long.

Max sure knew how to put a man down. And keep him there. The old one-two punch. Humiliate the poor bastard in open court and then turn on him with syrupy kindness.

The worst part of the humiliation bit was that all of it was true. It was true.

The one and only *Seaward* glided gracefully into Royal's area of perception. Hell, it was *moving*.

He turned back to the table, as much for graceful conversation as anything else, and asked, "Where is *Seaward* bound?"

"She's bound to ride that hook till the day I die, I guess," Spielke grumped, without looking up from his labors. "God knows I'll never get a chance to—"

"She's underway, Max."

The Man bounded to his feet and crossed to the parapet in two quick hops. His hands gripped the brick top of the wall and Royal thought for an instant that he was about to vault over the parapet.

"What are those idiots doing?" he yelled.

"Looks like they're bringing her in to the pier," Royal observed.

Spielke raced to the wall-mounted telescope and laid his eye to it. "Oh *no*!" he groaned. "No one's at the helm! She's on auto-pilot!" He swung about to scream toward the table: "Paul! Angelo! *Seaward* is running aground! Get down there and bring her to!"

The next few minutes at that point on the Mexican coast were a dizzying kaleidoscope of frantic happenings.

Briefly, Royal felt like a movie director on an extravagant location shot who had just given the "action—cameras" command.

Seaward was looming larger and larger, picking up speed as she came, bearing down on the pier toward which Too Bad and his boys were running an obviously hopeless footrace with the pace of events.

As his hired hands scampered recklessly down the steeply descending stairway, Spielke stood rigidly at the parapet, beating a soft and slow tattoo on the bricks with both fists, staring with hypnotic intensity at the advancing vessel.

In the background, a few hundred feet off *Seaward*'s quarter, a speedboat was executing a sharp power turn and making for deep water.

A half-mile or so beyond the speedboat, a small helicopter was churning low across the bay on a closing course.

Too Bad took the bottom flight of stairs in a single leap and ran onto the pier, the others trailing out behind him.

"They can't make it, Max," Royal observed quietly.

"They'll make it. They have to make it."

Not in the real world, Max. They did not have to make it. Royal knew that they would not. And Spielke must have known it.

The cruiser, with three men aboard, lurched away from the pier and had barely gotten clear when *Seaward* reached *landward*.

Like a slow motion replay, she smashed into the pier and rammed on through the flimsy structure, sending men and materials spinning crazily off to either side.

Nor had the cruiser escaped entirely. It was damaged and foundering, and the three men aboard were hastily abandoning the wreckage.

Royal heard a groan escape the Man's taut lips, and then *Seaward* landed totally and began climbing rock with a groan and a screech to eclipse all other sounds of that moment.

Just before the final crunch, however, Royal would have sworn he heard distant gunfire, a chattering sound such as an automatic weapon might make.

And he had glimpsed again, momentarily, the helicopter—much closer, now, and in a strangely clumsy attitude—falling, it seemed, toward the water. But he would not connect up that fragment of vision until some time afterward.

For now, the moment at hand was moment enough.

Seaward was aground on the rocks, her bow ripped and gaping, listing badly to starboard already—and her engines still laboring to drive her onward through the mountain.

"I'm sorry, Max," the actor said, because he really was—but not for the Man.

The boss was ashen, frozen at his post. "I don't understand," he mumbled. "How could such a thing happen?"

Royal could not say, but he was getting a pretty good idea. And whoever was responsible was certainly no shitbag.

He turned away from that agony and went back across the garden, through the house, and to his car.

And then he started laughing.

He giggled all the way home, and when he got there, he went straight to the bar and snagged a bottle and took it to the beach for a solitary toast to a singular event.

He drank to the guy who did it to Max the Man.

7: The Call

There had been no time for an appreciation of the events to landward. Bolan had barely dragged himself aboard the boat when he noticed the approaching helicopter.

His was the only small boat in that particular area, and the chopper was obviously making straight for them. It could be a perfectly innocent flight, of course. But he could not count on that, nor even allow it as a possibility, and he needed to know their intentions at the earliest possible moment.

"Make spray!" he commanded the lady at the wheel. "And keep an eye on that chopper!"

The powerboat leaped off and executed a tight arc westward. Bolan sent a final glance at the slowly moving *Seaward*. She was picking up headway nicely and maintaining that doomsday course.

Other things were now pressing his attention.

He went quickly forward for a binocular check

on that helicopter. It was a small bubble-top with three men inside—and, yeah, they'd altered their course and were dropping lower in a quick intercept path. As Bolan watched, the side hatch opened and a familiar object came into view. It was a rifle, tipped with a suppressor.

He yelled to the girl, "Maintain speed but hold 'er steady. We have a game."

She nodded and cast a frightened look toward the approaching helicopter.

Bolan hauled the Uzi off the floorboards and readied the chamber, then took a position at the gunwale, concealing the fierce little weapon as best as possible behind his leg.

The chopper bore in hard a'beam, no more than fifty feet off the deck, then hung there while its occupants eyeballed the two in the speeding boat.

They made the girl, but apparently that was all they made, judging by the casual reaction. One of the guys had a hand-held PA, and the initial approach was a soft one.

"Boat below—please lay to. Emergency situation. Lay to, please, Miss Canada."

Marty shot a despairing look over her shoulder to Bolan. The ruckus produced by the chopper, combined with the sounds of their own motion, made verbal communications impossible. Vision itself was difficult, due to the buffeting by wind and spray. Bolan shook his head at her silent inquiry and made a hand signal, calling for an abrupt change of course to starboard.

She responded immediately to the signal, the

speedboat cutting across the chopper's course to pass beneath its belly.

The boat came about in a tight circle, making a full power run toward the east shore—returning to the general area of the *Seaward*'s anchorage.

The yacht was halfway home now, and Bolan was again close enough to note the reaction from the top of the bluff. A fast-moving string of human forms was descending that stairway. Bolan shook his head at that and turned back to the threat from the air.

The bubble-top was closing quickly on the new course—and this one was a gunnery run. The rifleman was kneeling in the open hatchway. He began firing from about fifty yards out. The rifle was semiautomatic, as evidenced by the spacing of the rounds, and the targeting was pretty damned effective.

"Throttle off!" Bolan yelled, as his craft took two hits through the fiberglass hull.

Marty heard that command, and her response was instantaneous. From full throttle in a speeding boat to no power whatever produces a dramatic change in forward motion. Unlike a rolling object—and very much unlike a flying object—the hull of a speeding boat settles down quickly in its confining medium.

Bolan was braced and ready for the lurching slowdown, the Uzi up and ready. The chopper swooped on past—and, this time, in just the attitude Bolan desired.

The first burst from the Uzi hung a wreath

around the tail rotor, disintegrating it. With loss of the opposing rotational force, the craft instantly lost stability and began windmilling around its main rotor. It swung crazily across Bolan's bow, tilting and flinging the kneeling rifleman into the water as the pilot fought for control.

The next burst swept the cockpit, and that was the end of the air-sea battle. The chopper hit the water on its side, and dug in, and immediately disappeared from view.

Marty gave a strangled little cry and sagged against the wheel.

"We're shipping water," Bolan told her. "Let's go—but take it easy."

Her voice was distant and choked as she asked him, "Shouldn't we . . . look for survivors?"

"There are no survivors," Bolan said grimly.

His attention was drawn landward by an uplifting of sounds from that quarter. *Seaward* had just crashed through the pier and was beginning to climb the rocks.

"That was terrible, simply terrible!" the girl cried. "How could you do it?"

He was not sure as to which particular event she had reference, nor did it matter. He was performing for effect, not for applause. Nor even for gratitude, though it would not have been particularly out of order.

"Are you driving the boat or am I?" he asked coldly.

"I'm certainly not," she said in a muffled voice.

He pushed her aside and took the controls.

Half the naval base would be on the scene in no time at all, especially so if that gun battle had been noticed.

And the boat was taking on water at an alarming rate.

"Look for a good landfall," Bolan told the surly lady. "How's your swimming form?"

"Adequate," she replied dully.

Bolan hoped so.

He'd won the battle but lost a boat.

And maybe—yeah—maybe he'd lost a lot more than that.

JR was sprawled lazily in the sand, on the beach in front of his villa, quietly toasting the event of the decade and watching appreciatively the hullabaloo on the bay. Every boat in Acapulco, it seemed, was converging on the disaster scene. It was not, after all, just any old day that one could see a genuine marine disaster. Even the excursion boats would, no doubt, be loading up with the latest in Acapulco sightseeing.

In fact, the Catena-Puerto Marques ferry was already on the scene and standing to, along with a miscellany of yachts and runabouts.

The actor chuckled with a vision of Max's face, looking down on all that rubbernecking and chaos at his front porch, so to speak.

It could not, he reflected, have happened to a more deserving son of a bitch.

It was at this point in his reflections that JR

noticed the swimmers—a hundred yards out, maybe, slowly making for his pier.

It was not all that unusual to find swimmers at his beach. It was not, after all, *his* beach. All Mexican beaches are in the public domain. What was unusual about this particular pair was their distance from the shore—the fact that they were obviously coming from much farther out—and the apparent grimness of their effort.

Those swimmers were in trouble!

JR dropped his bottle and ran onto the pier, prepared not so much for heroics but to at least throw out a couple of life rings.

But then he saw that they were not in that much trouble. A man and a woman, they were using float cushions from a boat or . . .

Uh huh.

A picture had flashed across JR's mind—a still frame, crowded with a lot of confusion and high moment—a helicopter, a speedboat, gunfire.

A ball of mush was forming at the pit of JR's stomach. He turned his back on the swimmers and slowly retraced his steps along the pier, retrieved his bottle, went on to his patio, took a seat near the pool and a pull at his bottle. Then he sighed, went inside and got his pistol, loaded it, and returned to the patio.

They came up the steps a few minutes later. A gorgeous blonde in a fetching bikini, breathing hard and moving slowly on wobbly legs.

And the guy. *The* guy, yeah. Tall and powerfully built, a strong-jawed Clint Walker type, handsome, eyes of blue glinting ice—blowing a bit hard, himself, but steady as a rock.

The sodden clothing clung to him—and that wasn't all; a big silver auto clung to him, also, strapped to the hip on wide leather.

Biggest damn gun JR had ever seen, but it was still in the leather.

He stepped into the open and showed them his own pistol.

The woman went hurtling off to the side as the big guy executed a startlingly sudden whirling dive. The silver pistol was in his hand before he landed. He could have blown JR to kingdom come, that much was obvious. For some reason, he did not. He could have, yeah. The whole thing had caught JR flat-footed and open-mouthed— frozen to the trigger.

They stared at each other across the guns for a tense moment, and JR was surprised to hear his own voice telling the guy, "It's okay. You're welcome here."

That other voice was icewater cold. "Put the piece away."

The actor dropped his little .25 plunker onto a longue and said, "I know who you are. You're safe here, for the moment."

That big pistol was still looking at him. "Who's here?"

"Just me."

"No house servants?"

JR shook his head and managed a wry smile. "I was planning on leaving town."

"See to the lady," that cold voice commanded.

The guy stepped around Royal and went into the house. Sure, he had to check it out for himself.

The blonde was just lying there, eyes open, terrified, breathing like the approach of orgasm, maybe just too damned exhausted to move.

JR carried her to a longue. "I guess I know who you are, too," he told her. "Hang tight. I'll get you a jolt of tequila."

She clung to him, shaking away the offer, and managed a few breathless, urgent words. "Mr. Royal!—that man!—do you know who he is? That's Mack Bolan!"

"I know, I know," JR replied soothingly.

"He'll kill you! He's already—"

"It's okay, it's okay," he said, pushing her firmly back onto the longue.

"He *knew* this was your house! He came here deliberately!"

"It isn't my house, lady," JR said quietly. "And Mack Bolan can't kill me. I beat him to the job—long time ago. Now you just lie back there and cool it. I'll get something to warm your innards."

But he did not.

Bolan came through the doorway at that moment and said, "Royal!"

"Yeah?"

"My name is Bolan."

"Yeah, I get that."

The guy just stood there for a long, ripe moment—then he sheathed his weapon and said, "I need your help."

"You've got it," JR replied immediately.

Who ever said, he wondered, that you only live once. Already, John Royal was living twice.

8: The Sell

The distraught beauty from Detroit was bedded down in a guest room, sleeping off a powerful tranquilizer. Bolan and his host were seated outside—in the sun, where the waning rays could lift some of the moisture from Bolan's soggy clothing, while he belted coffee and devoured a tray of sandwiches.

"The lady doesn't like me very much," Bolan told the actor. "I'm not especially overjoyed with her company, either. I want you to keep her here until the hell subsides. It won't be long."

"It's probably the last place they'd look for her," Royal agreed. "But I can do more for you than that. Can't I?"

"Can you?"

"Sure. I know a lot of the secrets around this town. More than they think I do, anyway. They treat me like the village idiot. I'm not that, Bolan."

"I know you're not," Bolan told him.

77

The faint praise seemed to spark a desire to give something in return. The actor toyed with his cigarette as he said, "I, uh, the lady—I don't believe she dislikes you. She's just overwrought."

"It has been a rough afternoon," Bolan conceded.

"She's pretty clean, you know."

"No, I didn't know that."

"Yeah. Look, they use everybody they can, however they can. I came into it with eyes wide open. I was broke, a has-been." His eyes lost contact with Bolan's. "I guess, uh, with show people—we, uh, what the hell, for most of us, it's why we go into show business. We want to be loved, see. Not just by *some*body but by *every*body. Once you've had it, Bolan, it's a tough thing to give up. It's hard, going back to nowhere. The mob can make it very comfortable for people like me. But, see, I *knew* what they were doing to *me*. People like that lady in there, though . . ."

The actor shook his head and took a long pull on his cigarette.

"Naw, not them. I mean, not really. They see the glamour, sure, the constant flow of money, the excitement and all. But they never see the real shit. Know what I mean? They never really see it. Or if they do, they don't know what it is."

"How were they using Martha Canada?"

"Not they—*him*. Cass. He was a little strange you know. Did you know that?"

"Know what?" Bolan asked mildly.

"The guy was gay."

"No, I didn't know that. Does it matter?"

The actor shrugged. "Only so far as the lady is concerned. He was a closet queer. Know what I mean? Lived in constant fear that his bosses would find out. Very discreet, yeah. You'd never tumble, just to look at the guy, would you. The only reason I know is because he came to me to supply him. Imagine that."

"Why'd he come to you for that?"

Royal chuckled solemnly. "Well, I am a whoremaster, I guess. That's the practical effect, anyway. Naw—Cass didn't want just anything that came in off the street. He wanted introductions to cute Hollywood boys. We have plenty of those, you know."

Bolan shrugged. "To each his own. So what about Marty?"

"Window dressing, I'm sure. Part of the cover, that's all."

"He didn't use her in the recruitment of girls? Or in the placement?"

"Definitely not for placement, no. Cass had nothing to do with that side. As for the recruitment, I'd have to say probably not. He had the babe long before he drew this flesh assignment."

"You'd never met her before today?"

"Naw. He flashed her at us from time to time. But she wasn't in the know, and he didn't want to expose her to any of this. I think he was really trying to keep her out front, visibly clean, dumb and happy."

"Okay," Bolan said, accepting it.

"I'm not really a whoremaster, either, Bolan."

"So what are you, Royal?"

"Same as her, mostly. I mean I've never been a *procurer*. Window dressing, like her, that's been most of it. I do have contacts. And while I'm not as pretty as she is, I've got the glamorous name to hide a lot of shit behind." He grinned. "And I had this reputation, you know, for the girls. It all just sort of came together, in pieces. First thing I know, I'm the ringmaster and Acapulco is a staging area for the flesh routes. But, hey, this isn't two-dollar stuff they move through here. I'm just showcasing talent, get right down to it—providing the introductions and making people happy. I never saw any money exchanging hands—and I doubt that the girls ever did. But they live in luxury, have whatever they want, and get a pretty exciting life out of it."

"For a while," Bolan said quietly.

"Well, yeah—until the bloom of youth and beauty begins to fade. But, hell, that's the story in a lot of legitimate careers. Look at Hollywood, God's sake. But look, I mean, this thing I've been into, it's no white slavery bit."

"Except," Bolan said, prodding the guy a little.

"Well, yeah, there are those exceptions. That's the part gives me nightmares and cold sweats. As long as the girls play the game the way it's written out for them, well, I guess they have it pretty high."

"And if they don't?"

Royal sighed. "Tampico."

"What about Tampico?" Bolan asked, though he already knew.

"It's Algiers West."

"I see."

"They don't end well, Bolan."

"So they don't."

"Six of them are headed there tonight."

"By what route?"

"Company plane—a Lear jet. Comes in from Tampico every day at six. Courier run. Turns right around and goes back to Tampico."

"Courier plane, huh?"

"Yeah. It's part of the network. I don't know what the connections are, beyond Tampico. But there's a couple of VIPs arriving on today's flight. Mob guys."

"You're telling me this for a reason."

"Yeah."

"What is it?"

The actor took in a deep breath and let it escape with a loud sigh. "I'd like to spring those girls, that's why. So should you. You put them there."

"I see. The result of a sloppy afternoon, eh?"

"Right. Max is a very tidy man." Royal made another of those sad chuckles. "It's kind of weird, you know. Max has no reverence for anything, especially not for human life or happiness. I mean none. But I stood there and watched the guy cry big horse turds over that goddam fucking yacht. Can you beat that? He weeps for his fucking yacht."

Bolan sighed and said, "Yeah, I can beat it. I met a man once who wept for his soul."

"What does that mean?"

"Figure it out."

"Maybe I already did." The actor took a long look at his wristwatch. "It's nearly five thirty, Bolan."

"So it is."

"Will you go to the airport with me?"

"Yeah, I'll go. First, I need your telephone."

Royal's gaze flicked to the instrument. "It's all yours."

Bolan picked it up and dialed a local number from memory. He got a connection on the first ring. A Spanish-accented voice announced, *"Spielke villa."*

"Mr. Spielke, please. Mack Bolan calling."

"Momento."

Another voice came on almost immediately. It was a hard, no-nonsense tone. *"Who'd you say is calling?"*

"The name is Bolan. I'm not waiting forever, so trot the man out right quick."

"If this is a gag . . ."

"It's no gag. Get him."

"Hold on."

The actor's eyes were round balls of disbelief. He gasped, "You're the crustiest damn—"

Bolan shut him down with a wave of the hand as another instrument clicked into that connection. *"This is Spielke."*

"I sent you a yacht. Did you get it?"

"*You rotten son of a bitch!*" The voice was cold with controlled fury. "*What did you hope to prove by an insane stunt like that?*"

"It proved I could do it. Are you a believer, Spielke?"

"*I'd like to talk that over with you, Bolan. Face to face.*"

"You'll get your chance. I didn't call to taunt you, guy. I want to sell you something."

"*What is this?*"

"Call it a hard sell."

"*So what are you selling?*"

"I find the yacht market very boring. Think I'll sell houses."

There was a long silence on the line as the Man thought that one over. "*Just what is it you're saying?*"

"I have the fanciest villa in town wired for doomsday. If you want to buy it, I could take off the wires."

"*You're a lunatic!*"

"Maybe. But I'm pretty good with wires. If you're not a believer yet, I can show you another trick."

"*I don't think I'm following you, mister.*"

"I guess you're not. But you'll learn as we go along. I'm taking your empire apart, Spielke. I'll send you another piece of it within the hour. You'll be watching for it, won't you."

"*Wait a minute here! Let's understand—*"

"No, let's not waste each other's time. I can see

83

you're not ready for a hard sell. I'll send you another item of belief, then we'll talk again."

Bolan hung up and got to his feet.

He said to the actor, "Okay, let's go to the airport."

"Well wait. What was all that? Hell, I wish I could have seen his face. What did you mean?"

A faint smile pulled at Bolan's lips. "Well, I sent him a yacht."

"Yeah? So?"

"Now I think I'll send him an airplane."

"My *God*!" Royal exploded. "You're really serious, aren't you!"

"I have never," the big guy replied solemnly, "been more serious about anything."

Royal could believe that.

Yeah. JR was a believer, for sure.

9: The Fly In

By choice, Bolan really did not go in for cute stuff. He much preferred a militarily precise combat order and a straightforward execution of the war, but there did exist those certain situations, from time to time, which seemed to call for a bit of stunting.

Case in point: Acapulco.

There was no mob here, as such. Most of what was here was one man of vast wealth and impressive connections. Maximillian Spielke, and an idea—*La Nuovo Cosa Nostra*. The man was a naturalized Mexican citizen, respected in his community and seemingly securely affixed within the power structure of the country. The idea was a phantom network of power and ambition that encompassed the globe.

Spielke himself did not hold the patent on the idea; he was merely the executor. Acapulco was not intended to one day become the capital city of the New Mafia; it was more a Potsdam or a

Malta, the place where the idea would take flesh and form.

And, speaking of flesh, Acapulco was also the injection point for a dissemination of secret agents to police the new order, a Mata Hari corps which would infiltrate every level of world politics and commerce via the monied jet set. Many of these girls, Bolan knew, were unwitting accomplices to the conspiracy—until it became too late to extricate themselves under any conditions save death or total degradation.

And then there was the matter of narcotics. That scenario, as Bolan knew it, read something like this: The market for illegal drugs was becoming hotter with each passing year, not cooler by any stretch of wishful thinking—despite the almost frantic attempts at control by concerned nations.

What was happening, now, in the U.S. and other Western countries was very similar, both in national mood and in governmental actions, to the situation existing during the prohibition years in America. The people were determined to have the stuff and the governments were reaching that point where they were beginning to admit that they really could not control the situation. Alternatives to total prohibition were being sought. Many American states were already well down the road toward a decriminalization for the use of marijuana. Soon, went the reasoning, the dam against the harder stuff would also begin to crack, if only as a "law and order" measure.

But—one may ask—hadn't the repeal of prohibition in America wrecked the mobs which had prospered and fattened in the bootlegging rackets?

Indeed not. Those with vision and business sense had merely moved with their ill-gotten wealth into the legal trade. They already owned much of the production capability and had undisputed control over the distribution networks. They became even fatter, and used this new legitimate base as a springboard to sustain and cover other developing rackets.

Bolan did not have the full narcotics picture for the New Mafia, but he did know that their thoughts were running along those lines—and he did know that they were moving vigorously to consolidate their already powerful grip on the international traffic in narcotics.

And the question was definitely on the agenda for the Acapulco conferences. Bolan suspected an attempt toward formation of a narcotics cartel, similar to that forged by the oil producing nations.

There were indications, also, of actual movements of the stuff through the port of Acapulco. Those indications were nothing more than whispers and conjectures, however. Bolan had found no actual evidence of a thriving narcotics market here.

By and large, then, what he had in Acapulco was a phantom by the nostrils.

There was no "mob" to be attacked here.

He had to attack a *man*—and he had to do that in such a way that the *phantom* would die with the man.

And, yeah, Mack Bolan had met a man once who wept for his soul ... and nothing else. Not for the world or its problems. Not for his brothers and sisters, parents or children. Not for staggered institutions and the decline of human dignity, not for the loss of freedoms or the lack of justice ... not even for the loss of love and true respect.

There were people who wept only for their own miserable souls.

Bolan knew, now, that Max Spielke could weep for something. And the Executioner intended to introduce that guy to his own soul. He was going to show him something worth weeping for.

As they drove to the airport, he asked the actor, "How's the security at that joint on the hill?"

"It's something fierce," Royal replied. "He's brought in his army from the Costa Chica. They're swarming all over the place."

"Yeah, I have their number," Bolan said. "But how good are they?"

Royal shrugged. "All I know is what I hear. I've only encountered them twice. They look damned efficient to me. And I hear that they're crack troops. Modern equipment, fantastic discipline. I overheard Max remark, once, that he could subdue small nations with that force. Maybe he was just blowing, but it's not like Max to blow hard. I'll tell you something about that guy. He's a mean son of a bitch. And he always knows exactly where he's at and what he's doing. Frankly, I'm scared to death of the guy. He gives me certain leeway—because I think he really likes me, or at least he likes having me around. But he's mean as a snake." The actor sighed and took his eyes off the road momentarily for a quick glance at the strong profile of the man beside him. "He won't be easy to take down. I don't know just what you have in mind, but . . ."

"Fun and games won't do it, eh?" Bolan said quietly.

"I'm not trying to tell you . . ."

"It's okay," Bolan said. "You've put your life on the line. You know that. You have a right to speak your mind."

"My *life*. Big deal," Royal said bitterly.

"I can't promise you that I'm going to pull this off. I don't want you laboring under any false assumption that you've switched to the stronger side. There's—"

"Hey! If that's what you think—"

"I didn't say I thought it, guy. I'm just saying that you shouldn't. I operate most of the time on the short end of the odds. Because of that, I may seem a bit reckless sometimes. And maybe I am. But I'm never playing games. It's important that you know that. I get the idea you're stringing me along, you're going to be in a very dangerous position. Otherwise, I'll protect you all I can. But I can't even promise that."

"Did I ask for promises?" Royal huffed.

"Okay. Just so you know. What about the joint on the hill? Is there any type of electronic security?"

"Not that I know of," the actor replied thoughtfully. "They have two-way radios. And people all over everywhere. But if you mean electric eyes and stuff like—I don't think so. But listen, I can give you a layout of that joint, room by room and—"

"Thanks, I have it."

Royal's eyes raised in appreciation of that revelation. "How long have you been around here?"

"Long enough," Bolan assured him.

"How are we going to handle this, uh, thing at the airport?"

"We'll have to play the ear. You spot the ladies for me. I'll take care of their escort. You take care of the ladies. Take them back to your place, I guess, for now. We'll work out something from there."

"But, uh, you won't be coming back with us?"

"No. I'll be taking their place on the plane."

"Oh. Hell. Uh . . . what does that mean?"

"I told you, JR. I'm going to send the guy an airplane."

"Yeah, but . . . Uh, I mean . . . *how?*"

Bolan chuckled without humor. "The only way I know how. First rule of warfare, Royal, if you mean to win—don't hit their weaknesses, hit their strengths."

The actor laughed nervously. "Which means?"

90

"You tell me. What is Spielke's greatest strength?"

"Hell, I—the joint on the hill?"

"No. That's his weakness. It can wait. Right now, JR, I have to hit the phantom."

"The what?"

"I have to hit his strength, JR."

It was not a particularly impressive airport, by U.S. standards, but it was a very active one. Several U.S. airlines operate directly into Acapulco, as do Canadian and Australian flights. The Mexican lines, AeroMexico and Mexicana, provide frequent service to and from Mexico City, Puerto Vallarta, Guadalajara, and other points within Mexico.

Norte Americanos seemed to be the principal users of these services—and there were many of these in constant coming and going—but the atmosphere there was a truly intercontinental thing.

The Lear jet, with its *Compania Maximillia* decals in' modest display, was taxiing toward a special area reserved for private aircraft.

Bolan was wearing a new outfit from the waist up, courtesy of a local flying service employee—a hat which actually fit and a shirt which almost, with *Aero Acapulco* embroidered above the heart. All it cost him was fifty bucks American. Tossed in for free was a set of noise-blanketing earmuffs and the guy's job for ten minutes. The AutoMag had remained behind, at JR's villa. The .38 snub,

91

in leg holster, was all he'd need for this relatively simple task.

Royal's women were clustered at the service ramp, awaiting the arrival. They were dressed alike, in a sort of feminine uniform resembling those worn by flight attendants, and each carried a small, over-the-shoulder bag.

Waiting with them was a big Mexican in a tropical suit of impeccable white, packing a briefcase.

"Who's the guy?" Bolan asked his new partner.

"Cabrillo, one of the company couriers. He's always armed, so watch him."

"Think the girls understand what's happening to them?"

"Aw, no. They think they're off on a lark somewhere. They've been at Tres Vidas, the fancy country club hotel down here by the airport, ever since the shooting. Naw. Max handles this sort of thing with class. They won't know where they're headed until the door slams behind them."

"Okay, that's a problem for you," Bolan said. "You'll have to convince them, and get them out of here with minimum fuss."

"I can handle it," Royal assured him.

"Okay. I'll take care of the courier. Play by ear and take it from there. I want you off and moving before the fireworks start."

"Bet on it," the actor said lightly.

Bolan squeezed his arm and walked onto the ramp to direct the Lear to its unloading station.

He'd never done it before but he brought the

big craft right to its mark without a hitch—wondering, as he did so, just how much the pilots really needed this little act of guidance.

Two guys were in the cockpit, formally uniformed. He gave them a cheery wave and went around to position the stairway at the cabin door.

John Royal had made his approach to the group on the ground. The courier, Cabrillo, was engaging him in angry conversation, and the women were beginning to mill around the two.

Bolan stepped over and pushed inside the circle, conked the courier with the butt of his pistol, and told Royal: "Buzz off!"

The group flowed one way, Bolan the other. He was on the boarding steps when the aircraft door opened, and he was inside with the startled steward by the throat before the guy even saw him.

"Close this door!" he growled. *"No salida del avion! Comprende?"*

"Yes, I understand," the guy replied in perfect English. He understood the .38 in Bolan's big fist, too.

So did the guys in the cabin.

It was a plushy, VIP-lounge type of configuration with full-recliner chairs and all conceivable animal comforts. Full bar, conference table, the works. Four guys were in there, getting their stuff together, primping.

Everything froze for a timeless second when Bolan made his entry—but then time moved on and the two bodyguards must have thought it was on their side.

They went immediately for hardware. There was not that much time left in the world for either of them. The snub .38 crackled like a toy in Bolan's paw, spitting twice and spattering that lovely cabin with exploding life forces.

The other two cowered in a corner as Bolan collected the weapons. He motioned the attendant to a chair and shoved the VIPs face down on the cabin floor.

The door to the flight deck opened, and a startled face peered out.

Bolan shoved the guy back inside and held the door open, taking station in the doorway for equal visibility both ways. *"Vamos, de prisa!"* he commanded in cold and precise Spanish. "Do you read me, *Capitan?"*

"Hijack," the guy replied, with a lot of cool.

"That's it. Take 'er up. And let's have no cuteness with the tower. *Yo comprendo Espanol, Capitan."*

The guy was young, perhaps thirty years, and he spoke American-English like a native Angeleno. "Your wish is my command, mister," he replied coolly, with a glance at the carnage in his main cabin.

He was already cranking the engines. The copilot had not left his chair. He was a bit younger than the captain, and apparently spoke little English.

The copilot pulled on a headset and began a transaction with the control tower, in Spanish.

Bolan was not really all that great with the

language—but he could pick up key words and phrases.

"Hijack" must have become a part of the international language. The guy used it several times during his request for immediate take-off clearance.

The tower was haggling, hedging, trying to delay the departure.

"Tell them," Bolan said heavily, "to clear out the traffic. We're taking off. *Capitan*—your choice of runways."

The skipper sighed and began his taxi roll while the other guy passed the word along to the tower.

A moment later, they were airborne.

The guy was a good pilot—cool, steady, alert. "Where are we going, friend?" he asked.

"Head west," Bolan instructed.

"I'm short on fuel. Why don't I take you to Puerto Vallarta?"

"I said west . . . friend."

The cool was cracking, just a bit. The pilot glanced at his mate and tried it again. "There's nothing west but endless stretches of Pacific Ocean. Let's be reasonable. I simply don't have the fuel capability."

"We aren't going that far west," Bolan assured him. "Once we clear the airport zone, head west. Fly a two minute leg, then come about on a direct course for Puerto Marques."

"You fly planes, friend?"

"I fly whatever is handy ... friend. Right now I'm flying you. Start your move."

Bolan was certainly no pilot, but apparently he had the guy thinking that he might be. Which was okay.

They started out the west leg of the flight plan as the skipper inquired, "Okay, it's Puerto Marques for landfall. Then what?"

"We're landing there, friend."

"At Puerto Marques?" The guy laughed and poked his partner with an elbow. "There's no place to land at Puerto Marques," he declared, very patiently, as though speaking to a total cuckoo. "We *took off* from Puerto Marques, friend. Acapulco International serves this entire area. There isn't even a spot large enough to handle a Piper Cub at—"

"We won't be needing an airport," Bolan told him. He was beginning to enjoy the conversation. "We're landing at Villa Maximillia."

"Nuts," the guy said. "No way, man. I wouldn't try to put a helicopter down on that eagle's roost."

"You know the place, then."

"Sure. This is their company plane. Didn't you know that?"

"I knew it," Bolan replied. "But that's where we're landing, *Capitan*."

"No, see, you don't get it. There's no—"

"We're landing in the front yard."

The guy chuckled. "Yeah?"

"Yeah," Bolan said, chuckling with him.

96

"There's nothing out front but water, friend."

"That's right. What's wrong? Haven't you ever ditched a plane before?"

The guy looked at his copilot with a sick grin. "Get serious," he said to Bolan.

Bolan dropped a marksman's medal on him and said, "You get serious. It's going to take all the skill you have—but then I'm counting on you having a lot of that. Knowing Max, he wouldn't have a toonerville conductor handling his property."

The guy was fascinated by the bull's-eye cross. He showed it to his copilot and said, "Yeah, sure. You want an ocean ditch, eh?"

"Here's the way you're going to do it," Bolan instructed. "You'll make a straight-in approach, right out of the sun, low level. You'll set her down as close as possible to the shore. Unless you enjoy long swims in deep water at sunset, I suggest you get *very* close."

"What if I tell you this plane won't take a ditch?"

"Would it take a dive, better?"

"It's not a DC-3, you know."

"Where do you want to put it, *Capitan*? In the pond or on the patio?"

The guy let out a quivering sigh and said, "Okay. We'll do it your way. How many live passengers do I have left back there?"

"There's still a couple."

"How do you know they can swim?"

"I don't especially give a damn whether they can or not."

The copilot was whispering something into his headset. Bolan snatched it away and tossed it into the main cabin.

"Radio silence from here on," he commanded.

"Okay," the skipper said. "If you want to commit suicide, mister, okay."

"I guess I'm leaving that in your hands, aren't I," Bolan told the guy. "And it works both ways. Believe it."

The guy believed it.

He began explaining the situation to his copilot. Map cases opened, and the preparations for a ditching at sea got underway.

The *Compania Maximillia* Lear jet was heading home.

10: The Convincer

The noisy circus of curious onlookers had been efficiently herded away by the naval authorities and some degree of calm had returned. A covey of official boats remained on the scene, however, and a large crew of salvage workers swarmed the rocky shoreline directly below.

Seaward lay partially on her side, firmly aground and impaled upon an outcropping of jagged rock, the tide retreating around her, bow agape but—for now—that wound well above the waterline.

Bad news had just come up from the naval inspector, though—the yacht had sustained other serious structural damage along the keel line. It would be impossible to pump her out without first raising her and repairing the damage.

Spielke, watching the activities from above, groaned with that news and sent the word back: "Okay, let's get some securing lines on her so she won't slip away from us. I want a couple of barges down there, damn quick, to support the after section and keep her from breaking apart. Whatever it takes, do it. I got a couple of naval architects and a salvage expert on the way. Let me know as soon as they arrive. Oh, and tell Captain Gonzales I appreciate him sealing the area off."

It was sickening, just sickening—the whole miserable affair. Spielke's head was splitting and his guts were churning. Sick, yeah, he was a sick man. Somebody else was going to get sick over this, too—sick to *death*. And Max Spielke was going to stand there and *laugh* at that bastard's dying screams.

He turned to his chief lieutenant and snarled, "Did that jerk call back yet?"

"Nothing," Too Bad replied. "I think he was putting you on, sir."

"I want this town took apart! Are you reading me? I want that son of a bitch *found!* I want his *balls*, Paul!"

"It's just a matter of time, sir," the lieutenant assured his lord. "There's no way he's going to make another move without us knowing it. I got that description from Captain Padilla circulated all around, now. Cabs, buses, hotels, restaurants, cantinas—both sides of the bay, up and down and all around. We'll nail him."

"What about the helicopter? Any word yet?"

"No, sir. It went out, and it didn't come back. I guess those reports were true."

Spielke gnashed his teeth and snarled, "Okay!

That makes a yacht and a helicopter that bastard owes me! It'll take him a long time to pay, Paul."

"Yes, sir." Too Bad understood that. It was going to take Mack Bolan a long time to die. "I passed the word that we want him alive, if there's any way."

"You better believe it," Spielke muttered as he turned back to the parapet.

Another lieutenant hurried over to report, "Mr. Spielke, Cabrillo is on the phone. Something's funny at the airport."

"That's a break," the boss growled. "I haven't heard anything funny all day." He glanced at his watch. "He should be on his way to Tampico."

"Yessir, that's the problem. Cabrillo says he got mugged at the airport while he was waiting to get on the plane. Sounds kind of confused. You want to talk to him?"

"I got a headache, Juan. What the hell is . . . ?"

"Well, he says Royal was there and, I don't know, something about interference; they were having a beef about one thing or another, I don't know. Somebody, maybe Royal, I couldn't get it straight—somebody slugs Cabrillo. Next thing he knows, the plane is gone and he's lying there on the ramp and the airport cops are asking him a lot of questions. He sounds confused."

Another telephone rang, and Too Bad went to get it.

Spielke told the other man, "Handle it, Juan. Get the straight story and handle it. Contact the flight if you have to and find out if those broads

101

got aboard. Then make sure someone is at Tampico to take them in tow. And tell Cabrillo I said his story damn well better be straight."

Too Bad yelled from the conference table: "Boss! This is the control tower at the airport! They say our plane has been hijacked!"

Spielke put a hand to his forehead and groaned.

Too Bad said something into the telephone and hung up then hurried back to the boss's side. "Nobody knows exactly what happened," he reported calmly. "The plane came in from Tampico okay. Landed and went to the gate. They *think* nobody got on or off. But then the plane radios the tower and says they have a hijacker aboard. It took off and headed west. They still got it on radar. Say it's heading out to sea."

Spielke muttered, "It was *him*, Paul—*him!* He calls here with cute threats. So we draw in our defense line. And all the time he's lamming out of the country—with *our* plane."

"You think so?"

"Sure I think so. He was probably at the airport when he made that dumb call. And I fell for it. God, Paul, my head hurts bad. Did you say nobody got *off?*"

"That's what they think."

Spielke groaned again. "Hell, Lambrighetta and Zolotti were on that flight. He's got them, too."

"Uh, yeah, boss, there were gunshots just before the plane took off."

The Sultan was pressing both hands against his head. "Put in a call to General del Gado in Mexico City. Use my name, say it's urgent." The instructions were barely audible. "Let me know when he's on the line. I'll speak to him personally."

"That's, uh, the air force guy—right?"

"Right."

"You okay, sir?"

"Yeah, I'm okay. He's not getting away with it, Paul. I'll chase the bastard all the way to China, if I have to."

"I'll make the call," Too Bad said quietly, and went away to do so.

The *Capo Mexicana* turned his throbbing head back to the sea. Hell, everything had gone sour. It was unbelievable that one guy—a foreigner, operating alone on Max Spielke's own turf—could come romping in and, in a matter of hours, turn the whole thing completely sour. Unbelievable, yes. But it had happened.

Maximillian Spielke had always taken quiet pride in the knowledge that he was not a "made" man but a self-made one—and he had enjoyed making this fact known to visiting Mafia VIPs in various subtle ways. He'd taken virgin territory and moulded it into his own image, and he owned homage to no man. It was *his* territory, and he shared it with no one. The Italians strutted and sneered and played their silly games with secret societies and mock royalty; Maximillian Spielke ruled absolute, like the One God, alone and aloof, *allowing* the International Strutting and Sneering Society to play in his sunshine.

So maybe he'd allowed too much.

They had brought their problems with them as well as their golden opportunities.

And what did *Compania Maximillia* need of their wealth and their so-called power?

What did the Golden Land need of their *problems*?

He had quietly chided them, many times, for their weakness in the face of this Bolan *el Verdugo*, the fierce *El Matador* of their own making.

And now he was chiding himself for, perhaps, underestimating the threat of this man, for discounting the fabled prowess of this Mafia-stalker as more legend than fact. He had known how the Italians exaggerated, how they worshipped at the shrine of *image* and *reputation*. And he had dismissed the man Bolan too quickly, perhaps.

Yes, much too quickly.

It was perhaps just as well that the guy was gone. *Maximillia* could absorb the losses and go on as though the guy had never come. A scent of embarrassment here and there, maybe, but not enough to really weaken anything. If the guy had stayed and kept battering away—well, even though Spielke knew in his heart that he would get the guy sooner or later, a lot of damage could be done in the getting. Was the work of a life-time—a *self-made* lifetime—to be so recklessly spent?

The *Capo Mexicana* decided, then and there, that it was not. He was *glad* the guy was gone. Good riddance, and here was hoping he never came back.

His churning gut began to settle immediately, with that decision. He popped a couple more aspirins into his mouth and washed them down with flat beer, made a wry face at that, and signaled the hovering houseman for a fresh bottle.

When the guy brought the beer, Spielke told him, "Bring my stool, Pepe. I'm going to sit here awhile."

"The sunset, yes, it is *magnifico* today, sir."

The boss of Acapulco gave not a quick shit for all the sunsets in Mexico, though he was not likely to admit that to anyone. The sunsets were an Acapulco institution, not unlike a religious observance. Spielke didn't need it.

He settled back onto the "stool," a sort of high-rise recliner with footrest, and stared at the reddened skies without really seeing them.

The head was getting better, thank God.

Too Bad drifted over, with a clipped cigar and a ready lighter. The Sultan accepted the cigar and the light as the lieutenant reported: "They're trying to locate del Gado for you. He left the office early and nobody seems to know where he went."

"Forget it," Spielke muttered. "It's too much for too little."

"Okay, I'll cancel it," Too Bad replied, his eyes flaring with surprise.

"What's happening down below?"

The lieutenant took a quick look and replied, "Looks about the same. Sure is a mess, boss."

"It's insured," Spielke said, trying to come to philosophical terms with the unchangeable. "So's the helicopter. Those are the only losses *we* have had, Paul. Maybe we're lucky, at that."

"The Lear jet," Too Bad reminded sourly.

"We'll get it back. And if we don't—well, it's insured, too."

"I have a thought, Mr. Spielke."

"Yeah?"

"Maybe this Bolan guy is *not* our hijacker. We don't have any real facts, yet. I think we better keep the guard up."

"Oh, sure," the boss quietly agreed. His eyes were closed, fingers lightly massaging the lids. "Keep in touch with the airport, Paul. Let's stay on top of this thing."

"Yes, sir. I have Juan covering that."

Too Bad placed both elbows on the parapet and leaned out for another look below. The sun was a red ball just above the horizon, streaking the sea with several shades of red and casting long shadows across the bay from the west peninsula.

"Wonder if that could be our plane?" he asked whimsically.

"What's that?" Spielke muttered.

"I'm kidding. A plane is heading in, just under the sunset." A moment later: "Kind of low, though, isn't it? That's a big plane to be flying that low."

Spielke opened his eyes and took a look. He straightened up and took a closer look. "Bring me the glass!" he commanded.

Too Bad lifted the telescope from its mount and hurried it to the boss.

Spielke placed it to his eyes, fiddled briefly with the focus, then whispered, "Well I'll be damned!"

"Is it ours?"

"It's a Lear jet. *What the hell are they doing?*"

From the conference table, Juan's excited voice: "They lost radar contact! The plane is either down or flying just off the deck to avoid the radar!"

Too Bad exclaimed, "Holy ... ! They're going to buzz the house!"

"*Aw shit!*" Spielke screamed.

It had suddenly become very obvious that the plane was not going to "buzz" anything, except perhaps a few scurrying small boats in her path.

She hit the waves at about two hundred yards out and hydraplaned for another hundred yards or so before settling into her own backwash.

Huge rippling waves, produced by the disturbance, were moving onto the shore and making things a bit uncomfortable for the boats and shore party around the *Seaward*.

"That did it!" Too Bad yelled. "*Seaward*'s yawing off!"

But Max the Man had temporarily lost interest in prideful possessions. Neither the yacht nor the executive jet, as material objects, rated very high in his interior list of priority interests—not at this moment, at any rate.

"The son of a bitch," he commented in an awed whisper. "I don't believe it. He sent me a plane."

But he did. He believed it.

Max the Man had joined the ranks of the believers.

11: Death Hand

Yeah, the guy was a skilled pilot. The shock of impact came not too unlike a jarring landing on both feet after a leap from a rooftop, except that in this case most of the trauma was felt in the midsection.

Bolan was the first one to throw off the seatbelt and find his feet, though the cabin attendant was a close second.

The Mafia fatcats still had their heads between their knees and grunting with the shock when the pilot and copilot lurched into the cabin.

The steward had gone immediately to the hatch and thrown it open. Now he was fighting a limp inflatable raft, trying to feed it through the opening. The plane was tilted at an odd angle and settling fast; obviously it would not remain afloat for long.

Bolan tossed a silent salute to the pilots and stepped astride the open hatch.

"I'll get it," he told the steward, and paused

there long enough to pull the rubber inflatable clear and pop the cylinder.

The raft whooshed into shape and fell to the water. He passed the securing line back to the steward then hit the water in a clean dive, surfacing some twenty feet from the plane.

Bolan oriented himself to the shoreline then slid beneath the surface again and stroked strongly toward his goal.

When he surfaced the third time, for air and orientation, he was halfway there and the Lear jet was showing only its tail. The plane disappeared completely while he got his breath, leaving only the rubber raft and five somber silhouettes against the setting sun to mark the spot.

Night was coming with a swiftness, the shoreline already dusky and shadowed. Several boats were bobbing around the stricken *Seaward*, and there was a lot of shouting and scrambling about in that general vicinity.

A larger boat, something on the order of a naval frigate, was slowly making for the rubber raft.

Bolan went down again, and again, and then he was precisely where he'd wanted to be—in the midst of the confusion ashore.

Straining and groaning men were staggering around with lines and pulleys, trying to make fast a doomed yacht which obviously wanted only to rest in peace. Some of these guys wore a sort of rough uniform; most seemed to be Indians.

One guy stood out from all the others. He was

about Bolan's size and coloration, wore an Australian bush hat cocked at a swagger angle, and looked like a man with authority. He was soaked from the waist down, although apparently he'd not been handling lines; an assault rifle was slung from his shoulder. And he seemed to be headed toward the stairway to fantasyland.

In the confusion, what was one more soaked, exhausted human being? Bolan rose up out of the water and strode forward to intercept the Sultan's officer.

The guy turned to look at him just as Bolan unloaded one from the knees—and that one was all it took.

He dragged the unconscious trooper behind a rock and traded clothing with him. The assault rifle was a Russian AK-47, very similar to the M-16. Bolan's mind played idly with that fact while he got into the uniform. The blouse was a tuniclike affair, extending just below the hips and cinched at the waist with a braided belt. He cinched himself into it and cocked the hat at the same jaunty angle as the trooper had worn it, then he shouldered the AK-47 and sauntered up the stairway.

It was an impressive joint, yeah.

He paused briefly at the top of the stairs to get the lie and find an ear to play.

He had come not a'blitzing but a'looking.

There was plenty to be seen. A couple of servants in white outfits were setting up a buffet supper beside the pool. Lights were coming on, in various parts of the hotellike house. Another servant was moving through the garden area with a flaming stick, lighting hurricane lamps, or whatever—obviously for decoration effect; there was plenty of electric power available out here.

Six guys in casual civvies flanked an oval table with numerous telephones upon it. All were watching the buffet preparations with impatient appreciation.

The sun was fully gone, now—only its vivid rays making a spectacular light show along the horizon.

At the edge of the overlook, near a bricked safety wall, a chubby little bald-headed man sat quietly in an oversized chair. He was gazing solemnly out to sea, his back to the others.

Bolan set his ear and headed that way.

This edge of the soaring gardens was in semi-darkness. Potted trees and flowering shrubs of exotic dimensions suggested a jungle atmosphere —but the entire effect was man-made.

The little man turned to Bolan's casual approach. "Ramirez?" he queried in a tired voice. "*Que pasa?*"

Bolan swung the Russian rifle off his shoulder and leaned his back against the parapet. "It's not Ramirez, Max."

"Ah, hell," the guy said miserably.

The Bolan voice was icy, low-pitched, almost confidential. "You said you wanted to discuss something with me, face to face."

"This is nutty," the Man said, matching

112

Bolan's tone. "You've walked into an armed camp."

"Flew in," Bolan corrected him.

"Yeah. I was trying to forget that." He laughed quietly. It was the sound of a tired man who'd found peace with himself in that fatigue. "That plane looked big as an ocean liner when it hit the water. You've brought the navy and the tourists out again, Mr. Crazy. Now we'll probably never get them home again."

"Everybody likes a good show," Bolan said. "How about you?"

"Oh, sure. I thought it was thrilling."

"Take a stroll with me, Max."

"I'm not going nowhere. Neither are you. Soon as you make a move, two hundred savage *soldatos* are going to run right up your silly ass."

"I've been counting on it," Bolan told him. "But you shouldn't. Not with the muzzle of this Russian burper stuck down your throat. I doubt that your savages will get that anxious. Who would pay the bills with the Sultan gone?"

"Think you have the upper hand, eh?"

"I have the death hand, Max. That's the one that counts."

"You got a lot of nerve. I'll give you that."

"Call it desire. And, yeah, I have plenty of that."

The guy was looking him over, taking his measure. "I guess you have," he said, finally, with a deep sigh. "What do you 'desire' from me, Bolan?"

113

"I came for that talk."

"Really?"

"Yeah. But on neutral turf, not here."

"You think I'll just get up and walk out of here with you?"

"It's what I desire, yeah."

"Then you're out of your head. The only hand I got is to sit pat. Right? I let you take me out of here . . ."

"Start thinking, guy. If I'd wanted just your head, you think I'd come in here to get it? I have you wired, Max. Surely you know that by now. I can take you any time, any way of my choosing. I wouldn't choose this way."

"You wouldn't, huh?"

The guys at the oval table were getting to their feet and moving toward the buffet. It was chow time, and this seemed to be the priority item of the moment.

A big guy with beefy, sloping shoulders paused midway between the tables to toss an inquiry toward the shadowy figures at the parapet. "Snacks are ready. Can I get you something, boss?"

"Not just now, Paul," Spielke called back.

"Ramirez?"

Bolan waved away the offer.

The big guy went on to the buffet table.

Bolan congratulated his captive. "So you started thinking."

"Yeah, I started thinking before you got here,

114

Nutsy. I don't like all this trouble on my turf. I run a clean territory. I like to keep it that way."

"Too much to lose, any other way," Bolan agreed.

"Everybody loses," the Man said.

"The dirt got here before I did," Bolan pointed out.

"I been thinking about that, too."

"I don't want your turf, Spielke."

"I figured you didn't."

"I just want your borders closed."

The guy sighed. "Yeah, I figured that, too. To tell the truth, I'm kind of tired of this crap, myself. Never get a chance to enjoy myself anymore. What the hell have I worked for all my life?"

"Shut it down, then," Bolan suggested. "I'll go away happy. Your little *mordida* empire will have time for its daily *siesta*. And we'll all live happily ever after."

"How do I know you won't be coming back—just to play your sick jokes on a tired old man?"

"I've learned to accept some things," Bolan assured him. "There are those places where the game will go on, regardless of who's pulling the strings. Like Mexico. I guess I can't think of anyone I'd like to see in your place, Max."

"You mean that, don't you."

"I mean it."

"Well I think we're getting somewhere. You know something? You're a bright kid. Let me see what I got here. How many people did you kill today, on my turf?"

"I don't count," Bolan replied coldly.

"I do. Let's see—the navy has the plane crew and the spaghetti suckers, Lambrighetta and Zolotti. That means you burned two, there. Nobodies, they don't count—they're not mine. You let my courier go. You let my boat crew go. You let my man down on the beach go, and all his house staff, while you were burning Fulgencio and Scapelli. I, uh, hey—that's pretty clean. I lost just three men—those boys in the helicopter. You took them, huh."

"I took them."

"Ramirez?"

"He may have lost a few teeth."

"Yeah, that's pretty clean. I respect that. Okay. You got a deal."

"That's thinking," Bolan congratulated him.

"You won't shoot out my window glass or run any cars down off the cliff, huh?"

Bolan chuckled. "A deal's a deal, Max."

"Okay." The little man slid to his feet. "I'll walk you outside and get you a car. We had our talk after all, didn't we. You want to meet Paul and the boys?"

Bolan said, "Thanks, I'll pass. And you understand the deal isn't sealed until I'm home clean. If it should go sour . . ."

"It won't." Spielke took his arm, and they strolled casually through the gardens, the host pointing out various prideful possessions and talking chummily about the pressures of having and holding.

116

Paul "and the boys" watched with casual disinterest as the Man steered the Executioner through a vaulted doorway and along a short passageway which bypassed the main mass of the house and led to the parking area.

There, he summoned another Bush Hat and ordered a car brought to the gate, then he and Bolan strolled on along the drive.

Disengagement could be a tricky business, even when all intentions were entirely honorable, and Mack Bolan was not the last man in the world to understand it. He ordered the vehicle outside and parked just around a bend in the drive, all the guards inside with weapons stacked at a respectable distance—then he tossed his own appropriate weapon into the bushes.

Spielke chuckled and voluntarily accompanied him to the vehicle.

"Remember, we have a deal," the Man reminded him, as Bolan slid into the car.

"Let's call it a death-hand pact," Bolan said. "I'll have you wired for the rest of your life, Max."

"Or the rest of yours," Spielke replied, laughing, and went back up the drive.

Bolan drove away from there with a feeling of real accomplishment. He had not shaken their house down, by any means, but maybe he had succeeded in bolting all doors. He would settle for that, things being as they were.

He had tested the Man's *strength*, and found it resilient enough to accommodate an alternative to an all-destructive war. And he believed the guy was sincere; there would be no phantom *Cosa Nostra* operating from Mexico.

Yeah. Bolan was feeling pretty good about the whole thing.

But he did not know, then, what lay ahead of him along that brutal road to disengagement in Acapulco.

He could not have known, at that point, that the rampage had barely begun.

12: One More Time

Bolan was a man who respected his agreements and liaisons. He wanted to get back to John Royal and determine where the guy wished to go from this point, and to help him get there if he could.

And then there was the matter of Martha Canada and the six other girls. Bolan had purposely kept such matters out of his conversation with Spielke, feeling that the less said about the matter, the better.

But these were dangling considerations which had to be resolved before he could even contemplate a complete withdrawal from the Acapulco scene—and he had told Spielke that there would be "no deal" until Bolan was "home clean."

"Clean" included Royal, Canada, and the Tampico kids.

He took the Spielke vehicle to Hornos Beach and left it there, then doubled back on foot, *sans* bush hat and tunic, to his "hard drop"—a small villa in the hills above the east bay.

It was not plush, nor had it been advertised as such by the travel agent from whom Bolan rented it. "Budget villa" was the classification—and it fit. The stucco was cracking, the floors creaked, and the furniture was a bit tattered—but the place was clean, private, and entirely adequate for Bolan's quiet needs.

He had his weapons cache there as well as other necessities for survival in warfare, a varied wardrobe of clothing, miscellaneous gear for the tourist look, and a rented vehicle. He'd visited the place only twice during his stay in town; he hoped to tell it goodbye forever within a few hours, at most.

He showered and shaved and selected a wardrobe befitting the moment—dark slacks and open-neck shirt with black cravat, soft shoes and subdued socks. Next, he strapped on the Beretta shoulder rig and tested the action, then drew on a light denim sport coat and inspected himself in the mirror.

Finally, he dropped sunglasses into the coat pocket and went away from there.

He sensed something "off key" at the Royal villa even as he made his approach, which was customarily a cautious one, no matter how routine the event.

Royal's car was not present, for one thing. For another, there were no lights except for a couple of patio lanterns on the ocean side.

He went on by, and parked several hundred feet beyond the villa, near a public access to the beach. This was the quiet hour on the east bay, a time when most visitors were catching their breath from the daytime activities and preparing for the excitements of the evening. By eight o'clock, things would be humming again with fun and festivities. Right now, it was quiet, almost eerily so.

Bolan went to the beach and walked along the high tide mark until he reached Royal's, then made a quick pass over the wall and dropped into the shadows, senses and supersenses flaringly alert to the situation there. Both told him that something was definitely wrong. He moved on to the pool and showed himself in the patio light, lit a cigarette, waited, and felt the night.

Someone was in the pool.

He found the switch and turned on the underwater lights, then moved to the edge for a closer look.

Yeah.

The corpse wore white. He was on his back, eyes staring up at Bolan through eight feet of water.

"That's *One*," Bolan muttered and went on to the house.

True to the wriggly premonitions, he found *Two* curled on the floor in front of a couch in the game room. It was the one and only John Royal, hog tied and head shot.

A marksman's medal lay beside the body.

Bolan picked up the medal and inspected it closely, then dropped it into his pocket.

Royal's body was still a bit warm. There were powder burns very evident on the shattered head. A big piece had done it, at very close range.

He found the shell casing under the couch.

A *big* piece, yeah.

"I told you no promises, guy," Bolan muttered angrily.

He went to the cupboard where he'd stashed the .44 AutoMag—and, sure, it wasn't there.

How very neat.

The bed where Martha Canada had lain still bore her imprint—but the lady wasn't there.

An over-the-shoulder bag containing cosmetics and miscellaneous junk hung from a peg in the powder room—but the Tampico Kids were not there.

No one was there but Bolan and two men recently dead.

He returned to the pool for another look at *One*. There were no visible wounds. Probably the poor guy had simply been held under until the inevitable occurred, then released to find his own level in the depths. A Mexican male, in servant's white.

It was not quite eight o'clock. Two hours earlier, Royal had declared that he'd "sent home" all his help.

Where'd this guy come from?

Bolan was trying to find a time logic.

The drive to the airport had consumed some ten to fifteen minutes. Which meant that Royal and the girls could have arrived back at the villa at around 6:15 or 6:20.

Everything must have been okay, at that moment. Apparently he'd decided to call his houseman back to duty, and there'd been time for the guy to get there and die with his boss.

Why?

Bolan strolled to the beach gate and stared onto the bay for a moment. Suddenly he knew what else was "not there."

. One of the boats was missing. There had been two of them tied to the pier when Bolan and Royal left for the airport—a ChrisCraft cruiser and an outboard runabout. So now there was just the runabout.

He went on to the pier, walking slowly and looking for signs. And he found one. A fresh cigar butt, well-chewed and still soggy, was wedged between the footboards of the pier, as though someone had stepped on it and smashed it through the crack. Bolan left it there and went back to the house, recalling other "signs" in the game room which merited closer attention.

On a table near JR's body was a large ceramic ashtray, clean except for a long cigar ash and a small pile of burnt paper matches—burnt almost to the very tip, each of them.

He examined the body more closely, looking for burns.

There were no burns. But he did strike some paydirt in Royal's right fist. He had to pry the objects out of that death grip—and then he wasn't sure of what he had.

It was an empty match folder, with *Cantina Lola* imprinted on the flap.

Also a miniature replica, about an inch long, of the famed underwater statue off Roqueta Island—The Virgin of Guadalupe.

The matchbook, sure, that was easy. The burnt matches in the ashtray had been torn from that book. JR had known that his time had come. The empty matchbook was a message from a dead man.

But what was the Virgin of Guadalupe?

Bolan spent another ten minutes shaking out signs, and he found the biggy almost precisely where he'd started. The Royal villa was bugged—and damned cleverly, at that. He found the first wireless mike planted atop a bookcase in the game room. The rest came easy. Every room in the house was planted, even the bathrooms.

He went outside to look for the transceiver. There had to be one, and close by. He found it atop the pool house, a cute little package of solid state technology about the size of a cigarette carton.

It was a perfect setup. A boat could lay off out there in the middle of the bay and monitor that collector.

And even the patio had ears. He found that one cleverly woven into the fabric of the umbrella which shaded the very table at which he and Royal had sat and talked, a few hours earlier.

Spielke? Surely not. He would have known about the airport stunt in plenty of time to head it off.

Who, then?

Dark corners of the Bolan psyche were drawing in on the center. Who indeed? Who had the big stake in Acapulco?

Bolan went away from there very quickly, then, and pulled a lot of gyrations with the vehicle to make certain that no one could possibly be on his tail, after which he went looking for a public telephone with combat stretch.

He found one near a sidewalk beer garden on the Costera, and made his call. It took him awhile to get Spielke's ear, and he wasted no time with preliminaries when he got it.

"The deal is not sealed yet, Max. I have a question for you. John Royal. Did you burn him down?"

The Man sounded very far away. "Johnny? Burned?"

"All the way. Tell me a simple yes or no, and I'll believe you. He wasn't part of the deal, anyway. Did you or didn't you?"

"Course I didn't!" the Man fumed. "I don't even know what you're—"

"Know where all your boys are?"

"They're right here. We've been in a planning parley ever since you left. Nobody touches Johnny without my say-so. They all know it. I didn't say so, Bolan. What happened? Where are you?"

"Are those your bugs?"

"What? *What?*"

"Johnny's villa is lousy with electronic ears. You didn't know?"

A very long silence ensued, which Bolan himself finally broke. "I guess you didn't. Who do you think does, Max?"

The reply came as a mechanical monotone. "I don't know. But I guess I better be finding out."

"It's a new game, Max."

"I want no part of you, Bolan. Stay out of my hair."

"I'll try. I'm still looking to seal that deal, guy. It'll just take a bit longer, now. You still interested?"

"More than ever. Listen. Keep me posted. Will you?"

"Check your own joint," Bolan suggested.

"What?"

"For ears."

"Oh. Hell."

The line went abruptly dead.

Bolan grinned solemnly and returned to his vehicle.

There was a new game in town, sure.

The next move seemed to be Bolan's. And it sure as hell did not involve a disengagement from Acapulco.

Bolan felt it in his shivers.

A hard war lay directly ahead.

13: Clear Darkly

The ticklish task had required considerable maneuvering and several frustrating misfires, but Bolan had finally achieved the "clear" connection. Even so, it was necessary that the language be severely shaded.

The voice at the other end was that of Leo Turrin, the best kind of friend a man like Bolan could hope to find. Leo wore two hats, a white one and a black one—both with very high crowns. He was both a high-level federal cop and an almost-Capo with a powerful eastern family.

"Okay, this is clear," said the voice of friendship from far away. "Is it warm where you are?"

There had been no contacts since Colorado.

"Very," Bolan replied. "It's an international call, Sticker, so I don't know how many ears it's going through."

"Right, understood. How are things in Mexico?"

"Very interesting. When did you hear my arrival?"

"It came down a few hours ago, like little birds."

This could be highly important. Bolan asked, "Black birds?"

"Oh, both colors. Everybody's interested, Striker."

"That figures, but I'm just a bit surprised at the routes. I thought it was gift wrapped. Which flag flew first?"

"The white one," Turrin replied. "What time you got there, now?"

"Quarter to nine."

"Okay, the white flag went up at about five, your time. Black one a little before six."

"You sure it came in that order?"

"Positive. Is it that important?"

"Could be," Bolan told him. "Remember Butch Cassidy?"

"Sure do. How's it going with old Butch?"

"Bad. His horse died this afternoon."

"Hey, that didn't come," Turrin said quickly. "Are you sure about your information?"

"Very sure. I was there."

"Oh hell. Somebody might get unhappy about that. He was wired, you know, by big white daddy."

"Yeah, well, tell big daddy the wires had gotten frayed. I never agreed to those wires, you know. They were not cut casually, Sticker."

"If you say so, okay with me," Turrin replied

soberly. "I'll pass it along. Uh, what's happening now?"

"Damned if I know. It's why I called. Thought maybe you could tell me."

"No, hell, this is the first I've heard. The birds just dropped the spots, with no amplifying remarks. Come to think, that's kind of strange in itself, isn't it? Uh, we're all wondering what it's like, down there."

"Both sides are wondering, are they?"

"Yeah. What're you doing for excitement?"

"The usual tourist stuff. Shopping and sightseeing. Oh, we had a big private yacht run aground down here. Belonged to a local named Spielke. You hear of Spielke?"

"Oh sure. Damned thing just leaped out of the water, huh?"

"Something like that. Funny, the guy had all sorts of miseries today. His executive jet did just the opposite. Sort of leaped into the ocean. Right in front of the guy's house. You didn't hear all that?"

"Was this before or after Butch's horse died?"

"After. I think the horse race started the whole disaster kick. Spielke says to hell with it. He doesn't want any more racing."

"Oh yeah?" Turrin commented interestedly. "That's going to make someone *very* unhappy. Can you verify that?"

"You can take it as gospel—and I think someone already *is* very unhappy. I need to know, Sticker. Who's got ears on Spielke?"

"God, I don't know," said the voice from Pittsfield. "I never heard of any."

"Black *or* white?"

"You got it."

"Well tell me this. Who was riding with Butch Cassidy?"

"Riding *with* him?" Turrin paused to think that one over. "Well, let's see, you knew about the Rover boys. They been there a long time. I mean, you know, we discussed that way back—when? Motor town?"

"Right," Boland replied. "You saying they ride the international meets, too? Are they licensed for that?"

"Well, no, not really. But I wouldn't be surprised. Rules are made because you're expected to break them, you know."

"You saying he has an escort, wherever he goes?"

"No, I'm saying he *might* have."

"Could you find out?" Bolan pressed on.

"I can try. Will you call me later?"

"Let's say exactly four hours later. Can you make that?"

"I'll make it," Turrin assured him. "What else should we talk about?"

"Do the Rover boys have a close thing going with Pancho Villa?"

"You mean, with the Rover boys South? I, uh, in certain matters. Not these."

"I see," said Bolan. "Okay, where does that leave me? Where'd the white flag come from?"

"I'll try to find out."

"Thanks. Also look at the ears on Spielke."

"Pretty big ones, are they?"

"Oh, hell, monstrous. You could call him Dumbo and fly him anywhere."

Turrin chuckled. "I don't get in on *all* the fun, you know. But I can check around. If the ears are there, I'll find their daddy."

"We got a real attraction down here," Bolan said chattily. "You ought to look into it. It's called the Virgin of Guadalupe."

"Hell, that's remarkable," Turrin said. "How old is she?"

"You do that with a capital V and a capital G. It's a big statue, under the water."

"What the hell's it doing under the water?"

"Got to give the people in the glass bottom boats something to look at, dummy. Anyway, would you look into that for me? It could be very interesting."

"A statue, huh?"

"Yeah. I think it has a hidden meaning."

"Uh huh. Okay. I'll put it on my list of things to see. You have any good gossip for me? Something to make me popular?"

"Blacks or whites?"

"Either or both," Turrin replied, chuckling.

"There's plenty, but I just don't know how to put it delicately, Sticker. It maybe should save for later. Here's one, though. You could tell big white daddy that the Central American horsemen went down with Butch—the first and second spots, that is."

"Oh. Really?"

"Yeah. And, uh, tell him also that it's very clean around here, from what I can see. I mean I see no movements, no pollution of any kind. Except in the mouth."

"Uh huh. All right. That about it?"

"For now, yeah," Bolan said.

"Okay. We have a date for, uh, one o'clock, your time."

"Don't fidget if I'm a bit late. I don't know what I'll be doing at precisely one o'clock. It's a swinging town.".

"Like that, huh? Okay. Watch your swinger, guy."

Bolan chuckled. "With both eyes," he said, and broke the connection.

When he went to the desk to settle the charges, the girl asked him, "Deed your connection make clear?"

"Very clear," he told her. "Yes, ma'am, it was very clear."

Very clear, yeah—but what exactly had it changed in the know and don't-know departments?

Trot them out and count them up, swinger.

Okay. He knew that the FBI either might or might not have been keeping Cass Baby under close surveillance while out of the country.

He knew that the New York boys might or

might not be the ones wearing electronic ears in Mexico.

He knew that "Bolan contact" reports had sped along both the federal and the underground alert systems, and that somehow the feds had known of Bolan's Acapulco presence a full hour before the mob knew.

Surprising? Sure. It was a land built for surprises.

Finally, he knew that he was in a hell of a bad tactical position—the very worst, from Bolan's disciplined combat point of view. He was shadow-boxing in the dark, and for a man with the whole world on his ass, that was—yeah, right—the very worst of all positions. Like wearing a blindfold and boxing gloves to an orgy. You could find a tangle, sure, but God only knew where you'd end up in the daisy chain.

As both a lover and a fighter, Mack Bolan was a man who preferred to call his own shots.

He'd have to be doing something about the tactical position, and very quickly.

Or, maybe, lose it all to the phantoms of Acapulco.

14: Virgin View

Bolan left his car close to the Costera to invade the red light district on foot. It was an interesting and "atmospheric" section of Old Town, with its dives, brothels, strip joints, and after-hours clubs.

Most of the brothels doubled as cantinas, and every cantina was a brothel. So, incidentally, were the dives and strip joints.

It was a bit early yet, and the district was relatively calm. In a few hours, the whole place would be in high tempo, though not reaching a peak in certain quarters until three or four o'clock in the morning. Some places blasted on until eight and nine.

Mexican authorities traditionally prohibit female tourists from entering such districts at any time of the day or night, for whatever reason. In Acapulco, it was a bit different. "Straight" couples were welcomed, even encouraged, and several of the clubs in this quarter of Acapulco had attained true "in-scene" status, especially for the after-hours crowd.

Cantina Lola was not, however, one of these latter. It was a dive, straight on. Dark, grimy, smelling of accumulated human sweat and stale beer. There was a short bar, near the door, and a few small tables, juke box and a tiny, raised stage—rooms upstairs and a door leading somewhere rearward.

The guy behind the bar was the only person in evidence. He was about forty, wore faded but clean Levi's and a crisp white shirt. He was bright of eye and quick of smile.

He greeted Bolan like a longtime friend. "What you doing so early, mon? No jukin' for another hour."

Bolan eased onto a stool and told the guy, "Thirsty, mon."

"Cerveza?"

"I guess," Bolan growled. "You got Carta Blanca?"

"No, mon, but I got Bohemia and Moctezuma."

"What's that Moctezuma?" Bolan asked, though he already knew. "The dark stuff?"

The bartender was already serving it up. "Try it, you'll like it," he said, smiling. "Ten pesos, mon."

Bolan threw out a ten and growled, "I can get it for seven on the zocalo, mon."

"Sure but you don't get the atmosphere there."

Bolan looked around the joint and chuckled. "You can say that, yeah."

135

"You want some girls? It's a little early, but I bet you fifty I could get a lineup down here in two minutes flat."

"Later, maybe," Bolan replied, still chuckling.

"You from L.A.?" the guy asked.

"No, but I've been there."

"Me too, mon. Three times." He held up three fingers as proof. "You know Alvera Street?"

"Good old Alvera street," Bolan said.

"You're packing a piece, aren't you, mon? How come you packing? Looking for some action?"

Bolan gave the guy a cold stare as he said, "You didn't spend all your time on Alvera, did you."

"I know a mon with a piece when I see one, mon."

Bolan stuck a cigarette between his teeth and asked bright-eyes, "Know a match when you see one?"

The guy reached under the bar and flipped out a book.

Same one, yeah.

Bolan lit the cigarette, allowed the match to burn to the edge of his grasp, then dropped it on the bar.

"You like the Moctezuma? Pretty good, huh?"

It tasted like sorghum molasses kicked with gin. But Bolan said, "It's okay." He lit another match.

"What you doing, mon?"

"Playing with fire," Bolan replied quietly.

"Looking for a connection?"

"Having a beer," Bolan said.

The guy laughed and turned away, busying himself with the setup at the back bar. Without turning around, he asked, "Where you from, mon?"

"I didn't ask you that, mon," Bolan said casually.

The guy laughed again. "Who you looking for?"

"A deaf and dumb bartender," Bolan replied sourly.

It broke the guy up. All up. When he turned back to the bar again, the Virgin of Guadalupe stood beside Bolan's beer.

The bartender's laughter abruptly ceased. "You like dolls, mon?"

"I like virgins," Bolan explained.

The guy laughed some more, but his heart was no longer in it. "Every girl we got here is a virgin and sweet sixteen," he told the cold-eyed customer. "You want me to find you one?"

"Just one, yeah," Bolan said.

Gone was the merry eye and innocent smile. The guy was hard and direct as he snapped, "Stay right here!" He whirled away and went quickly toward the rear.

Bolan waited until the door back there closed behind the guy, then he followed.

He was about halfway there when the door swung open again and two gringos in shirtsleeves and shoulder leather came charging out.

In the background, beyond the doorway, Bolan

got a snap impression of a small room with minimal furnishings and the bartender talking to a tall, gorgeous blonde in a mod slack suit.

It was no more than a flashing glimpse, and it was all the look he could afford to spend on background scenery.

The two guys in the doorway were brandishing their hardware. That confrontation was occupying the major share of Bolan's attention and directing his instincts. The Beretta snapped up at full extension, three quick rounds leaping out and striking faster than scrambling reactions could command a pair of slow trigger fingers.

The two went down loudly and grotesquely, with much flinging and spattering of fluids.

The door behind them immediately slammed shut.

Bolan leapt over the mess and kicked the door open.

"I'm clean, mon!"

The guy was standing against the wall, hands clasped atop his head and the legs spread wide, old habits dying hard.

A sharply dressed leg was just disappearing behind a low window sill at the back wall.

Bolan ran past the guy and followed the leg.

It was a very dark alley, mon.

He hit it cautiously, immediately catching the motion at the end of the building. A moment later, he received another half-glimpse of the woman as she disappeared around the corner onto the street.

It was glimpse enough.

He'd found the Virgin of Guadalupe, yeah—
also known as Martha Canada, girl adventurer.

And, God, how he hated that.

15: The Watch

He gave her plenty of rein and let her run. The narrow back streets of Old Town were busy enough to make the track possible, not too choked with people to defeat it.

She moved with confidence, only rarely glancing over the shoulder, circling surely toward La Quebrada then down the hill to the *zocalo*. He watched her hail a horse-drawn buggy at the Montera and head south.

Bolan crossed over and followed on foot, keeping the buggy in view but giving it plenty of head.

This part of town was in high gear, thronged with tourists and a full contingent of hawkers, vendors, and the usual variety of sidewalk merchants. It was a good night in Acapulco. The sidewalk cafes and beer gardens were enjoying capacity crowds, with dancing under the stars and miniature golf also getting a big play. Music from the *Fiesta*, a bay cruise boat, drifted across the water to add to the frivolous atmosphere.

All of which made the track a bit more difficult. Bolan was still quite a distance to the rear when the *calandria* pulled over, just below the yacht club, and the girl hopped out.

He closed fast, and picked up that golden head again as it moved purposefully along the line of docked boats.

A Mexican youth, who had obviously been awaiting the woman, snapped to at her approach. The two of them stepped immediately into a small dinghy.

A racing sloop, built on Salem lines, was riding anchor about fifty yards out, dim light showing at the cabin ports. The dinghy headed straight for the sloop. Bolan watched the woman board, then he strolled back to the yacht club office.

He passed a fifty-peso note to the guy on duty there and told him, "I'm supposed to meet some friends for a little party but I can't find their yacht. Can you help me? It's the *Mariah*."

The fifty disappeared quickly as the guy consulted his log. *"Si,"* he said thoughtfully. *"Mariah* has come in today from Zihuatenejo. She is—oh!—this is why you no can see. She is anchored just off—come, I will point—"

Bolan stopped the guy. "Don't bother, I'll find it. That *is* Señor Brown's yacht, right?"

The guy showed Bolan a blank look. "But no," he said, glancing back to the log. *"Mariah* is owned by Señor Cassiopea."

"Oh, I guess Brown is just using it."

"But no, señor. There is no Brown with *Mariah*."

"Well who checked her in?"

"Señor Cassiopea, himself."

Bolan was showing the guy baffled eyes. "When was that?"

"Six o'clock, señor."

"Today? I mean, this afternoon?"

"Si."

Pretty good going, Bolan was thinking, for a guy who'd been splattered all over JR's patio at *two* o'clock. He told the man, "I'm sure he said *Mariah*. Do you have a *Maria*?"

The guy blinked and his eyes swept the log book in a purely perfunctory exercise. "No *Maria*, señor."

Bolan sighed and peeled off another fifty-peso note—four dollars, American. "I just assumed he meant the yacht club. *Gracias*."

"*De nada. Momento, señor.*" The guy had integrity. For the extra fifty, he was about to make a call. "I will check the harbormaster."

"It's okay, forget it," Bolan said. "Uh, this *Mariah*." He made an embarrassed chuckle. "My friend Brown wouldn't be just one of the crew, would he?"

The guy again dutifully consulted his log. "No Brown, señor."

Bolan's eyes were following the guy's finger as it moved across the entry. He could not make out the names—but they would probably mean very

142

little, anyway. He was going for numbers, and he counted four.

"What's her port of registry?" he asked casually.

"Long Beach," the guy read. "California, USA."

"That's not my *Mariah*," Bolan said regretfully. *"Gracias* again."

He went out of there with more questions than answers.

The Mexican government took a very dim view of improperly registered foreign boats. There was a very precise protocol to be observed, precise registry at all ports of call, strict accounting of crew members. You left each port with the same crew who brought her in, or your boat would end up impounded for months or even years while the authorities decided what had gone wrong.

There would be no blatant oversight of that protocol by a wiseguy with a sensitive job to perform. If the log said four crewmen were aboard, then very likely that's what was aboard.

But, dammit, who *were* the people on that sloop—and why were they here? What had they been doing at Zihuatenejo, a sleepy fishing village a hundred miles or so up the coast?

Obviously, Cass Baby had arranged some sort of schedule for the *Mariah* to put into Acapulco at this particular point in time—and with his own name officially entered in the visitors' log.

Why?

Nothing in the guy's background indicated an interest in sailing, nor had *Mariah* been mentioned in any of the background material on the guy.

Martha Canada obviously knew the story.

So what the hell was going on?

Bolan hailed a cab and returned to the *zocalo* to pick up his car, then drove to the yacht basin and parked within view of the *Mariah*, settling into the watch with determined patience.

He had to find some answers. And he had to find them pretty damn quick. Bolan had well learned, however, that patience was often the quickest bridge from nowhere to somewhere.

He would wait and learn . . . and perhaps live to wait and learn again, another day.

Mack Bolan did not enjoy the dark thoughts occupying his mind during that long vigil beside the bay. He was a hard-nosed realist, sure, but even a guy like Bolan needed some optimism to cling to. And he did not like what was happening to his few fragile ideals concerning American womanhood.

Marty was obviously buried in this dark business all the way to her pert little chin. If the obvious should become established as the undeniable, then that lovely young lady was a direct contributor to the death of John Royal, as well as to the undisclosed fate of the six young women who'd been with him just prior to his death. Aside from the cold hard fact of murder itself, there was also the sickening odor of duplicity and betrayal.

Like it or not, he'd been affected by the lady. Yeah, and he did not wish to believe the things that were clamoring for belief.

Royal had been a weak man, sure, but not a rotten one. The guy deserved better than what he got, especially if you remembered that he died at the hands of one whom he'd selflessly sought only to protect—at great danger to himself.

Bolan had to believe Spielke, primarily because the tracks and the odors supported that belief. And if Spielke hadn't done it, and if Martha Canada was running around the city in the company of some very hard dudes ...

The Mata Hari corps, yeah. It did not belong to Spielke. Certainly it had not belonged to soft and easy John Royal. Was it led, then, by a blue-eyed "virgin" with a soul so dead as to turn on a harmless guy like JR and blow that guy away while he was tied like a Christmas turkey?

Yeah, possibly.

The lady had never been particularly warm to Bolan, but was it mere coincidence that she'd become so openly hostile only after their arrival at the Royal villa?

Coincidence, no—of course not—not for someone who *knew* that the whole joint was planted with electronic ears. Coincidence, no, for someone whose chief interest was to provide some interesting words for those listening ears.

Had she actually taken the sedative? Probably

not. Something like that was simple to fake. How long, then, had she been theoretically "alone" at the villa? Thirty to forty minutes?—from the moment Royal and Bolan departed for the airport until Royal returned with the other girls.

What kind of horrendous setup had JR and the six girls walked into, on that return? What was waiting for them there? And why?

Worst of all . . . who had helped to set the poor guy up that way? Who, indeed. "I need your help," Bolan had told the guy. And the response had come back quick and positive: "You've got it."

They were not comforting thoughts, no, those that accompanied the man during that dockside vigil.

There were several trips of the dingy, during those two hours—a bit of coming and a bit of going—a conference of conspirators, one could say.

And Bolan patiently took their note, numbering them and classifying them, marking and sizing them, until the last sour note had been sounded.

Then he followed the basic note, a coolly composed young woman, when she came finally ashore and stepped into a cab.

He smiled grimly at its destination, a *casita* at Las Brisas, a very familiar *casita*, one for which Mack Bolan had paid the rent.

He watched her inside, and saw her settle in, then he broke the patient watch and returned to Old Town.

Interesting, yes—even if discomfiting.

And now *patience* had run its course.

All that remained was the cross-check with Leo Turrin—and then patience would have its reward.

And then, very probably, one hell of a firestorm was going to rage across this lovely city on the bay.

16: Flowing Together

Bolan reached the telephone exchange a few minutes behind schedule, but this time there was very little delay in getting the call through to Leo Turrin.

"It's your southern correspondent," Bolan told that worried voice in Pittsfield. "What do you have?"

"I'm not sure," Turrin replied. "Sometimes I think the more I hear the less I know. Maybe it'll mean more to you than it does to me. Can you think of any reason why several large hunting parties would want to be at a place called Oaxaca?"

"Depends," Bolan said, "on where they came from and what they're hunting for."

"Yeah, well, they came from little old New York and thereabouts. I'd say they're looking for big game."

"Along the Costa Chica, maybe," Bolan tried.

"Is that where the black Mexicans live?"

"By and large, yeah."

"That's the region, then."

"I see," Bolan said. "Okay. How many you make?"

"Three parties, about fifty in each."

Bolan whistled softly. "Well organized, is it? Guides and all?"

"You got it," Turrin replied. "I make it about, uh, no more than a few hours from Acapulco. Less, if you're thinking in terms of air transportation. And I did hear something about choppers. Why do you suppose?"

"How does it sound from your end?" Bolan countered.

"Doesn't sound like much of a fun vacation," Turrin said sourly. "The other guys have it better, I'll bet."

"Which other guys?"

"The fishing parties."

"We have those too, eh?"

"Oh, sure. About four of them, scattered along the coast down there. These names mean nothing to me. Maybe they will to you. I read one at Puerto Escondido, one at Puerto Angel, another at Salina Cruz—then I got one I'll have to spell, I don't know how the hell to—"

Bolan said, "Zihuatenejo."

"Okay, if you say so. How'd you know?"

"That party has already arrived in Acapulco Bay."

"Oh. Well, the others could have moved too, I guess. I don't know just how close to the moment all this is. I had to pull it out of a—well, never mind."

"I understand," Bolan told him. "I guess these, uh, parties know how to keep in touch, eh."

"Oh, they're connected, yeah. Believe it."

"That good, eh?"

"Bet your life on it, buddy," Turrin said soberly.

"Okay, I'll do that. What else did you make?"

"How'm I doing, so far?"

"Four point oh," Bolan assured him.

"If you say so, okay. What else? Okay, here's an item. White daddy is very disturbed with you."

"Sorry to hear that," Bolan said drily.

"He says your ground is quote highly sensitive unquote. Thinks you should move on to a better vacation spot."

"I'm sort of attached here," Bolan growled.

"You're your own man. He said pass it. I passed it. Forget it."

Bolan said, "I already did. But tell daddy I respect his feelings. It's just that mine are what I live by. Or die by."

"Sure. No sweat," said the faithful friend. "I struck out on your virgin, I'm afraid. Nothing. But here's some other stuff. First, the flags."

"Okay, go."

"The white one was hoisted by a Rover boy detail in Washington. Get this. It came to them via the State Department. That's as far as I could get."

"What sort of detail is that, Sticker?"

"Something special. I couldn't get it."

"Okay. But you confirm the time. It flew at five, Acapulco time."

"Right. Now the black one. It came in on the New York express. I talked to the guy that took it. Are you ready? It originated from a ship at sea."

"How romantic," Bolan wryly commented.

"Yeah. It was a radio telephone hookup via RCA."

"Okay, thanks, Sticker. Maybe it's starting to come together. That, uh, special Rover detail. Could they be using associates?"

"You mean like foreign connections?"

"I mean like whatever," Bolan replied. "I just can't read Rovers in this picture down here. The smell is wrong. I need your feel on this, friend, for a very special reason which I can't go into here. What's your feel?"

"How about Rover mercenaries?" Turrin suggested.

Translation: FBI informants, unencumbered by the "law of the land."

Bolan said, "Okay, that smells possible. It's worth a thought or two, anyway. By the way. I've had six lost loves down here, already."

Turrin's voice sounded a bit out of it as he replied, "That's the price of valor, soldier."

"Well they're lost but not forgotten. Have you heard anything?"

"The number is *six*, huh?"

151

"One half-dozen, right."

"You lose 'em in bunches, don't you. No, I haven't heard. It's the sort of thing that comes as pure gossip, and usually much later. They don't talk much about lost loves up here. I mean, like, it's too lowbrow. But I can hang another ear out, if you'd like."

"Never mind," Bolan said tiredly. "I've got about all I can handle, as it is. You know a guy named John Royal?"

"Who doesn't?" Turrin replied immediately.

"Play a song for the guy, Sticker."

"Aw, no. Really? Were you there?"

Bolan sighed. "No, I wasn't there. Someone tried to make it look that way, though."

"What the hell is going on down there!" Turrin said angrily.

"There simply isn't time to tell you, friend. What'd you learn about Spielke's ears?"

"Just a confirmation of what you told me," reported the incredible two-headed marvel from Pittsfield. "They're definitely on—but get this. They're both white and black. You figure it, friend. Put it together with everything else, and I guess you've got some kind of heat going down there, pal."

"Oh, we have plenty of that," Bolan assured him.

"Don't get too close to the flames, Striker."

"You know me," Bolan said quietly, and killed the connection.

Flames, yeah. Like from several blowtorches all flowing together.

It was confirmed. This town, yeah, was going to be engulfed in a firestorm. Unless Bolan could stop it.

And he hardly knew where to begin.

17: Night Sounds

He was dressed in the blacksuit—the fabled skin-tight night combat outfit which had become such a symbol of the man and of his war. Even the hands and face were touched up with a black cosmetic. The gunleather was black, as was the weapon itself—the standard "quiet piece," a nine-millimeter Beretta Brigadier, dubbed the *Belle*, loaded with hi-shock Parabellum rounds and equipped with a unique silencer engineered by armorer Bolan himself.

He left all extraneous gear in the vehicle and moved into the night as a moving extension of the darkness. The moon had set, and the stars were filtered by scudding islands of fractured cumulus playing above the mountains.

The time was two o'clock. This end of the town was quiet. Occasional voices, raised in laughter and merriment, drifted across the quiet waters of the bay. Gentle waves lapped at the docked boats, slapping softly with unsteady rhythms.

Bolan slipped into the water and swam softly to the *Mariah*. He rested himself on the anchor chain and listened for the sounds of that small world, placing his ear to the wooden hull and working his way aft. There were no sounds from within, and no lights—but certainly something aware and conscious was aboard that boat.

He spotted the guy then. Topside aft, lying out on the deck with a pillow beneath his head, one knee raised and fingers playing upon it in time to some inner music.

Bolan took the lookout from behind, sliding up out of the water with a nylon garrote poised into the attack. He brought the guy with him as he settled back into the water, holding him there until the grimly silent struggle found its inevitable end. He removed the garrote then, and let the guy sink as he quietly hauled himself aboard.

The deck hatch was open. He lowered head and shoulders into the utter blackness of that tiny cabin and tarried there a while as his senses peaked into an absorption of that dark hole.

Lungs in motion and the occasional restless movement of a limb were the only perceptions of a full one-minute vigil, then the blackness began gradually separating into faint patterns of spatial structures. He identified a small cookstove directly below and to the right, a bunk to the left along the bulkhead. Another blob farther forward slowly resolved as another bunk—and, just beyond it, a bulkhead athwart ships. Beyond that forward bulkhead should lie another small compartment with extremely low overhead, suitable only for stowage or sleeping.

He lowered himself to waist height, then flipped on inside, landing lightly on his feet. The noose found its second victim in the first bunk aft. The guy died straining into total darkness and hearing perhaps nothing more than his own tongue vibrating against the roof of his mouth and the soft slapping of bay water against the boards beside him.

The one amidships did not even struggle. He simply rolled his eyes up into his head and settled quietly into the final darkness.

Bolan then returned to the small galley section, found a match and lit it, discovered the battery-driven lantern clipped to the bulkhead and turned it on.

He stood silently with the lantern behind him, allowing his eyes to adjust to the dim but relatively harsh light.

The forward cabin featured a sliding panel for a door. It was fully open, to allow maximum flow-through of air. The decking in there equaled about knee-height of the main cabin. A bare foot was showing in the open hatch. It moved, and a muffled voice complained, "What's with the light, babe? Aw, no! It's not four o'clock already!"

Bolan moved forward and seized the guy by the ankle and dragged him out of there. The guy hit the deck of the main cabin with a crash and a howl. Bolan stepped back to the rear, hauled out the *Belle*, affixed the silencer.

"I'll kill you, you screwy—!" Sleeping beauty was fighting mad. He was a powerfully built guy in his late twenties, wearing only jockey shorts. Sweat-matted hair was thick across his chest and down his belly.

He had come to his knees, prepared to beat the hell out of some jokester, when he became aware of the tall figure in executioner black. Then he saw the bug-eyed corpse in the bunk beside him—and he knew, he knew.

A small metallic object sailed the length of the cabin and dropped to the deck at his knee.

"You know the choices," Bolan said in an icy, impersonal tone.

The guy took a deep breath and held it for a moment before slowly letting it out.

Yeah, he knew the choices.

There were but two—life and death. The mere fact that he was alive and looking at Mack the Bastard was evidence enough that the choice was open.

The guy stared at his hands for a moment, then he sighed and dropped onto his butt. "Okay," he quietly decided.

Bolan reminded him, "I'm not a prosecutor and I'm not a cop. I'm just a guy with an ear for the truth. The minute I hear otherwise, the truce is over. And there will be no second thoughts or 'I forgots.' So go."

The guy went—calmly, quietly. He'd chosen life.

"I'm Renato. Pete Renato. I'm by way of Mike

Talifero—the late Mike Talifero, as you know. I don't decide these things, I just do them. Okay. The men decided. You know—the men, the board. They put it together this way, see—nobody else can run Mexico so smooth. We need Max. We need him. But he acts like he don't need us. He's getting tougher to handle all the time. So this is the way it went together. We take him down to size, that's all. We make him need us."

"You kill the kingdom but leave the king."

"You got it."

"But it went sour."

"Thanks to you, yeah. Threw off the timing. Max calls in his army. He's got an armed fort up there now. All we found in the boonies was a village of women and kids."

"That's very sad."

"We thought so."

"So you're trying to cool it now. How long?"

The guy shrugged. "I don't make those decisions. Until the army goes home, I guess."

Bolan said, "Until you can catch them asleep with their women and kids."

The guy shrugged.

"Why Royal?"

"I swear I don't know. I think that was a foul-up."

"Who fouled up?"

"I swear I don't know. That was all done before I got here. I asked no questions. I was told no answers."

"You don't like taking orders from a woman, either."

The guy gave Bolan a strained look and a level reply. "No, I don't. But I don't make the decisions. I just do the doing."

There were limits to these "truth truces"—limits which were largely proscribed by the man himself. Bolan had learned to respect those limits. He got more, that way. Some men would die rather than humiliate themselves or violate their own deep codes of personal honor. This man had gone his limit.

Bolan growled, "Go back to bed, Renato. Come dawn, all your troubles will be over. If you're a real wiseguy, you'll play it that way."

"My mama didn't raise any dummies," Renato replied calmly. He gave Bolan a limp salute, crawled back into his cabin, and slid the panel shut.

Bolan extinguished the lantern, stood quietly in the darkness for a few seconds, then rejoined the night.

He did not have it all. But he had enough.

At least he now knew where to begin.

18: Stage Center

"Did I get you out of bed, Max?"

"Fat chance," the *Capo Mexicana* growled. "I told you to stay out of my hair, mister."

"I made you a deal, Max, and I'm trying to keep it. Don't make it any harder for me than necessary."

The Man sighed heavily into the telephone. "What the hell is going on, Bolan?"

"It would take a book, and there's no time to retell the history of the world. I have to change the terms of the deal. You'll have to cash out completely. Out of the country, Max, for good. I think you'd like Rio. You'd feel right at home there."

"You're a real nutsy," the Man replied disgustedly.

"I thought we had this understanding," Bolan said drily. "I thought you'd learned to believe in me, Max. If I say it, you can believe it. Right?"

"Just like the One God, huh?"

160

"I don't claim to be infallible. But I know my business. I'm telling you the only way I can honor my deal with you is for you to leave the country. If I have to spell it out for you . . ."

"Why don't you do that?" the boss of Mexico said faintly.

"They're taking you over, guy."

The Man laughed bitterly at that. "They're welcome to try, rooster."

"They're already trying."

"So I'm ready. Send them."

"You don't have the picture, Max. They're going to burn just your kingdom, not your throne. They'll keep you there, guy, with wires all over you. They pull an arm wire, you salute. A waist wire, you bend over and kiss ass. Have that picture?"

The guy laughed again, but the mockery was a bit uncertain, this time. "Why're you so kind to me, Mister Nutsy?"

"It's not because I love you so," Bolan assured him. "But I do worry about you, Max. I can't honor the deal if you're not going to be your own man. I'll have to burn you down, sir. Once they get their wires on you, it will be too tough to do that. I'll have to do it now. Tonight, I guess."

Bolan had expected a blustery royal outrage at that kind of talk, but it seemed only to set the guy's mind.

"You're very serious about this," the Man observed quietly.

"Everything I do is very serious," Bolan told him.

"You think they're going to make a puppet out of me, eh."

"I-know it. I'll tell you a professional secret, Max. They've got three head parties down on the veldt right now—a very hard force, with all the machinery it takes to sustain it, and their bayonet is poised above your village at this very moment. Other parties are standing by along the coast, ready for a clean sweep inland. They've got you outgunned and outflanked. I'm a soldier, guy, and I can tell you: they've got you by the balls. All they have to do now is squeeze down and you're out of the game."

"How do I know this is—how do I . . .?"

"I thought I'd made you a believer," Bolan quietly reminded his listener.

"Okay. Let's say I believe you. Let 'em burn the damn veldt all the way to the coast, I don't care. You saw my people. They're here, with me. Let 'em try my hill, Bolan."

"You think it's a standoff?" Bolan said. "Think again. They can afford to sit and wait, which is what they're doing. You would have gotten wired tonight, though, except for me. I danced in and rearranged the stage a bit. Except for that, your army would be on the veldt right now, and they'd be waking up at dawn beneath the bayonet. You'd be waking up with a whole new palace guard— and fully wired. So now you put yourself at their table, Max. What would you do now? Rush the fort? Or burn the village and take hostages. Force the sultan's army out of the fort—via desertions, if nothing else. Your mestizos and Indians, Max—how long will they squat inside those walls with their wives and kids over the bayonet?"

"Aw, shit," the Man commented raggedly.

"It's no Mexican standoff, you know. It's a sure thing. So, you see, I have to ride with the sure thing. They'll get their wires on you, okay. I have to either pack you off or burn you down, Max. You can understand my position."

"You go get yourself screwed," the guy growled.

"Okay. Just so we understand it. By the way—did you find the bugs?"

"Go to—yeah, I found some. So what?"

"So how do you think they got there? Where did Too Bad Paul go tonight, Max?"

"He went nowhere."

"Sure he did. Ask him about the *Mariah*—and a guy named Renato."

"What're you saying?"

Bolan gave a theatrical sigh as he replied, "You surprise me, Max. How does a *Capo Mexicana* get so naive? You think I'm the only guy in town who might decide to ride the sure thing? Don't be too hard on the guy, though. He's just playing the game the way it was written. You could ask him, also, about the Cantina Lola. I think that's been their field headquarters for the past few months."

"It's been going that long?" the guy asked tiredly.

"Longer, probably. You've been around, Max. You know how long it takes to set up something like this. All the meetings, the quiet wheeling and dealing, the offers that are just impossible to refuse. You know, Max."

Sure. Max knew.

"You think I should bail out, huh. Well don't *you* be naive, mister. And don't *you* try me again, either."

"We have no deal," Bolan announced, and hung up.

So okay.

Another stage setting should begin to materialize very quickly.

Bolan gave it about thirty minutes to the first curtain.

He marked the time on his quartz chronometer, and set off for Las Brisas. It was time to mount another stage.

19: The Lady

The terraced hillside was softly enfolded in the quietness of the hour, totally darkened except for the small nightlights placed along the walks and drives.

Bolan went through the hedges and tried a soft recon of the interior situation. All the draperies were drawn, the total closure lessened only by a soft illumination at the bedroom window.

He went to the front door and quietly used the key to let himself in. The room was dark, empty.

From beyond the closed bedroom door issued the soft sounds of Mexican music—muted, hardly audible—from the bedside radio, probably.

He moved silently across to that point and carefully opened the door.

A small lamp on the nightstand was providing the illumination.

She lay on the bed with both pillows propping her head high, a partially eaten tropical fruit in one hand, eyes closed.

And she was raw naked.

It was, yeah, one hell of an electrifying sight.

The door to the bathroom was closed and no light was showing beneath it, but water was running in there.

Bolan stepped inside the bedroom and pulled the door shut behind him, deliberately producing an audible click in the mechanism.

Those eyes flew open and she stared at him through a momentary silence as the gaze swept his full length a couple of times. Then she kicked both legs and dropped the fruit, arms raising to him in warm welcome.

"I was afraid you wouldn't think to look for me here," she declared huskily.

He stayed where he stood as he replied, "You were afraid of that, eh."

"Oh, wow, that is a groovy outfit. It's really far out." She seemed to become only now aware of her own nudity. "Oh! Am I embarrassing you?"

"Not at all," he assured her. "But you'd better see to your bath water."

"I bathed," she told him, running both hands along that glistening torso as though to call attention to the cleanliness awaiting him there. "The thing is broken. Let it run." She patted the bed. "Sit down and tell me what you've been doing."

He saw the AutoMag, then. It was leathered and belt-wrapped, lying on the floor beside the bed.

He went over and picked it up, sprang it and

checked the action, then restored it to leather and carried it to the dresser, where he set it down.

"Thanks for taking care of Thunder for me," he said quietly.

"I figured you left it for me," she told him. "And I do appreciate it. I was scared to death, Mack. Really scared."

He said, very quietly, "Yeah."

"You're mad at me. Why?" She patted the bed again. "Let's bury that," she suggested.

"It's buried," he assured her. "Where were you when JR went down?"

Those lovely eyes flared and the gaze went abruptly down. "That was horrible. I was—I was—I can't talk about it, Mack."

"Try," he said harshly.

Those eyes blinked at him, hurting, pleading.

"I have to hear it, Marty."

She sat up and clasped herself in her arms, as though trying to keep it all together. "I was outside. In the pool. When the men came, I mean. I hid beneath the diving board until they left. I-I didn't have anything on. And I hid beneath the diving board until they left. Then I-I went inside . . . and then I saw it. And I panicked. I just ran away, Mack. Oh, God, I needed you. I was so scared."

"You hid in the pool, eh."

"It seemed . . . the smart thing."

"What time was this?"

"Oh, just—just—I don't know. I woke up feeling very down, you know. Very out of it. The sleeping

167

pill, I guess. It seemed that I was the only one there. And I thought a swim would bring me out of it. And so I . . . did."

"And you found Thunder when you came out of the pool."

"Yes."

"And came straight here."

"Yes."

"You didn't go into town, first, and buy a pretty new slack suit. You didn't go to the red quarter for a meet at Cantina Lola. And you didn't go from there to the *Mariah* for another series of meets."

That face was absolute innocence, bafflement, and abused feelings. "I don't know what you're talking about. I told you. I came here. Hoping you would think to look for me here."

The magic of the place was still there. Bolan was finding it very difficult to firmly establish the undeniable.

He stepped to the bathroom door and pushed it open. The lights were off and a couple of damp towels lay just inside the door.

He hit the light switch and pushed on inside.

The magic left that place, then, flung free by a great lurch of Bolan's stomach.

"Oh, no," he groaned, and tossed a sick look over his shoulder to the beautiful lady on the bed.

Another gorgeous blonde was in that bathroom. Also naked. But in a hell of a shape.

She lay on her back, in the tub—legs elevated, lashed together and tied to the shower plumbing, hands tied behind her. The bathtub drain was open, but the effluent was not quite keeping pace with the influent; that tub was slowly filling. The cold water was running full force through the shower head, which had been adjusted to play a steady stream onto the girl's face.

She'd taken quite a battering from that water, besides which she had little more than a nose to go before total submersion—and already she was snorting and struggling in panic.

Bolan turned off the water and cut the cord at her feet to haul her out of there. He lay her gently on the floor beside the tub and removed the other bindings. A rolled-up stocking had been jammed into her mouth and lashed in place with its mate.

She was only about half conscious, but she knew where she was and what was happening. He rubbed and patted her to further the consciousness, then helped her roll to her side and made sure that she was breathing okay.

"Stay loose," he told her. "I'll be right back."

Marty was standing at the dresser, the big silver pistol up and looking at him. She was holding it with both hands, bent slightly forward with legs spread apart the way they teach you on the shooting ranges.

The AutoMag was designed for a man with a big hand and a strong pull. It was not a lady's weapon, simply because there was not stretch enough in the normal female hand for a comfortable trigger pull and for most ladies, even the athletic ones, not strength enough to properly handle the fantastic muzzle velocities developing in front of that pull.

Bolan figured, with all that, he was spotting the lady to an even chance.

He coldly told her, "You had the world and all its magic, Marty. Why did you blow it?"

Big Thunder roared and bucked, staggering her, its 240-grain missile crunching into the floor three feet under and two feet wide on the left.

"It's a big difference from ten feet out, isn't it. Come and lay it against my head, Marty, the way you did it to JR."

She tried it again, with even worst results, then threw herself toward him with an enraged scream.

He blew the lady away then, with a quiet little chug from the *Belle*. It caught her at mid-stride and squarely between the eyes, expanding immediately to lay that whole beautiful face open, punching her back and flopping her down.

The AutoMag hit the wall behind Bolan.

He went to one knee to retrieve the piece and stayed there for a moment—then rose up with a weary sigh.

Soul-weary, yeah.

So much for feminine idealizations.

So much, also, for equality between the sexes.

The other blonde was leaning weakly against the doorway to the bathroom. "That bitch!" she gasped. "That lousy bitch!"

"Not anymore," Bolan said quietly. He turned

a somber eye that way and asked her, "Who are you, honey?"

"I'm Angie Greene," she replied, still seething. "I'm with the FBI, Bolan, so you keep your lousy paws off me."

He showed her a small smile and told her, "Now that's what I call a lady."

20: The Man

"So I lied a little," the shaken beauty admitted. "I'm not an agent. But I do make reports."

"A paid informant," Bolan suggested.

"Call it what you like. I work for a living, the same as everyone else."

"And you were working on John Royal."

"Right. This jerk bitch got the wrong slant. She thought JR was the leak in the plumbing."

"So why did you wind up in the bathtub?" Bolan asked.

She made a face and said, "Call it dumb devotion to duty." She delicately shrugged her shoulders. "Or to JR, maybe—who knows? He whisked us away from that airport, and we were headed back to his villa. Then he decided that we girls should not hang around any longer than necessary. He was really a sweet guy, did you know that? Well, he got out of the car a short distance from the villa and told us to go on to Mexico City, leave the car, and take a plane back to the States.

The other girls did that. I started to. But then after we'd gone about a mile, I jumped out and walked back to the villa. Straight into hell."

"They'd been waiting for him," Bolan guessed.

"Yes. Shortly after I got there, poor Carlos blundered in. They took him outside, and I didn't see him again."

"Carlos was . . . ?"

"Part-time houseboy."

"They drowned him in the pool," Bolan informed her.

"The rotten *bitch!*" she spat.

"Marty was the queen lady, huh?"

"It's pretty obvious, isn't it. Listen. *Cassiopea* worked for *her.* How's that? She was the control. He was a nothing, a front, a cover."

"Yes, that's kind of weird," Bolan agreed.

"For the mob, it sure is. Champs of the male chauvinist league. But there's a new wind a'blowing across our land, Mr. Bolan. Or hadn't you noticed."

Sure. Bolan had noticed. Women were showing themselves as equal to men in almost every sense. Even in savagery.

"Win a few, lose a few," he muttered.

"Does that mean good or bad?" she asked archly.

"Good, in your case," Bolan told her. "They need to make you a full agent. Tell them I said it. You beat the mob's alert by a full hour."

"What do you mean?"

"You put out the location report on me, didn't you?"

"Yes, I did. For all the good it—I mean—okay." She showed him a winning smile. "Nothing personal, huh?"

He sighed and said, "Nothing personal, Angie. Except for that, I might have never tumbled to the lady. I knew she figured somewhere, but I was trying to fit her into your role. But none of the numbers computed. There was no way she could have run up the flag before six o'clock. And six o'clock is when the mob's flag went up the pole. That gave me a lot of discomfort."

"You must have a pretty good telegraph system yourself," the girl commented.

"The best," he said, giving her a sober show of teeth. "Why didn't you, uh, tell the lady what she wanted to know?"

"I told her every damn thing I knew, and a lot of things I dreamed up on the spur of the panic. The dizzy bitch! I think it gave her kicks to truss me up that way."

"Girl adventurer," Bolan said sadly.

"You kind of liked her."

"Kind of. For a little while."

"I'm sorry."

"So am I." Bolan brushed the girl's forehead with his lips and told her, "Okay. This is the place. Get in there and lock every door and window. Call the American consulate—or whoever your contact is—and don't move a muscle or even sigh loudly until they come for you. Got that?"

"Got it," she said. "Thanks, Bolan. I'll never forget you."

She kissed him full on the mouth and quickly took her departure.

And, yeah, that's the way it was.

Marty had been the "controller." In charge of the bedroom detail. She had a couple of torpedoes based in Acapulco, as well as at other strategic points around the globe, to back her up and provide any needed muscle.

And apparently she'd been doing all right. Even Cass Baby was playing the second fiddle, and he was a guy high on the visibility list. It had not been Marty's fault that things suddenly soured along the New Mafia trail. She'd been riding high and handsome until the inevitable events within her dark world began to conspire against her. Very probably she had not even known of the furtive movements against the Spielke clan until she suddenly found herself enmeshed in them. Even then it would have been smooth sailing— and probably even more power for herself—if Bolan had not stumbled into the thing via his own bullish plans for the Mexican empire.

Maybe she'd just panicked and overreacted. That was one of the problems inherent with girl adventurers. They simply did not have the background for violence, and there was no way to condition them for the shoot-out.

Bolan did not know, nor did he really care, where she'd stood *vis à vis* the head parties from New York. She had good representation at the council, apparently. Perhaps the visiting hoods had simply been told to observe protocol—to work with the lady in every way possible so as to not unduly compromise her own operation in the area.

No, Bolan really did not care about any of that.

It was behind him, thank God. That which lay ahead would seem like a busman's holiday in comparison. He was a soldier, not a detective. And a soldier's job was awaiting him.

He drove on around the bay and up the hill toward the Throne of Mexico. The wrist chronometer beeped at him as he reached the check point and pulled into the bushes.

And, yeah, the timing was very close.

He'd figured about thirty minutes was the time required to break that camp, to load the trucks, to lay the plans and execute that tactical withdrawal to the Costa Chica. It was a military outfit, after all, and Bolan's own military mind was rather well attuned with like minds everywhere.

There was very likely to be a shooting war on the Costa Chica, unless Bolan's own timing worked to invalidate the necessity or sanity of such a confrontation.

Such considerations did not, however, particularly interest the man in black. He sought primarily to simplify his own task. The rest would take care of the rest.

And, yeah, he still had a job to do in Mexico.

The point truck rumbled through the gate and down the drive, and the military parade began.

He did not wait for it to end, but used that exodus as a cover for his own entry onto the palace grounds.

Big Thunder rode the honor spot, at right hip. *Belle* was snuggled into the left armpit. And that was all of his personal weaponry. It was all he could afford. Heavy packs at chest and back occupied the balance of his load capability.

A few of the troops, probably hand picked, had been retained as a skeleton palace guard. They were spread much too thin, of course, and posed no real problem to a penetration expert such as Bolan.

He was over the wall and deep into the grounds before the final truck of the convoy lumbered through the gate. He knew exactly where he wished to go, and he had at least a fair idea of the best way to get there.

It took him less than ten minutes to outwit the physical security of the place and to arrive at his goal. Then it required an hour to read the stress points and make the proper applications from the stuff in his twinpacks; another five minutes for setting the detonators, properly sequenced for a "staggered go."

He left the empty packs behind and hoisted himself onto the overhanging gardens.

"I figured you'd come," the Man said softly as Bolan dropped over the parapet.

It was dark out there—very dark. Bolan could have been no more than a soft shadow upon the night. So the guy must have been sitting there quite a while in that darkness, waiting for him to show.

"You're a true believer," Bolan congratulated him.

"Well, you sent me a boat, didn't you. Then you sent me a plane. I just couldn't wait to see what you were going to send me next."

"An ocean," Bolan quietly told him.

"A what?"

"I came to send you an ocean, Max."

"Aw, shit. I don't think you can do that."

"The mountain wouldn't come to Mahomet, Max."

"So Mahomet went to the mountain. So what?"

The sultan was on his throne, at the parapet, barely visible there, a shotgun resting casually across his lap.

"I'm not going to no fuckin' ocean, mister. I'm going to burn you down. Right here. Right now."

"You're already on your way to the ocean," Bolan told him.

"What's that mean?"

"I put charges on the mountain."

"You put what?"

"I gooped your mountain, Max. In a few minutes, the whole crazy fantasyland will fall into the sea."

The guy was a believer, yeah.

And he'd placed his love in more than a yacht. He lost his concentration for one staggering heartbeat, those shrewd eyes flaring into the rising recognition of a truth and seeking reassurance in the physical object of his love.

Bolan burned him with the silent *Belle* as those eyes swept the beloved gardens. Quick and clean, death flew faster than any possible signal of pain or reaction, and the *Capo Mexicana* slid from his throne without a murmur of protest.

"God save the king," Bolan muttered—and went in search of loyal subjects.

He found Too Bad Paul facedown in a potted plant, blood from a slashed jugular feeding rich nourishment there.

And he found a couple of other guys with fear on their faces and hardware a few sad millimeters too far removed from frozen fingers. "Relax," he told them. "The Man is dead and the joint is set to blow. There's nothing left to fight over, so get everybody out—and I mean especially the servants. All the way off the hill and as far as you can get. *Do it!*"

The guys did it, racing into the interior and setting up a clamor.

Bolan went back through the gardens and to the parapet, onto the stairway.

He looked down from there and wondered briefly what went through the minds of the miracle divers of La Quebrada as they flung themselves from heights such as this.

Then he went on down, the hard way, onto the small rocky beach below. An Indian with a ragged headband, the lone sentry left at that post, gave him a strange look but offered no challenge.

Bolan asked the guy, *"Comprende Espanol?"*

Not everyone did, in this land of many languages.

But the guy nodded and replied, *"Si, poquito."*

"Vamos!" Bolan advised. *"Retumbo-retumbo!"* He pointed to the cliffs. *"Comprende retumbo?"*

"Boom-boom!" the guy replied.

"You got it, pal. *Vamos!"*

Bolan walked into the water and started swimming. He swam straight out, as far and as quickly as lungs and limbs would take him, without rest, and then he crushed the compressed air cartridges in the belt at his waist and allowed the flotation to take over, turned onto his back, and continued the withdrawal at all possible speed.

He was about two hundred yards out when the first *retumbo* shook the night.

The others followed in close sequence, cutting that whittled headland into a series of stepped slabs with all the cantilevers dissolving.

The gardens went to the ocean first, sliding as a single piece onto the sheer facing, then breaking up and tumbling in leaping fragments of a kingdom in quick destruct.

Level by level they came, grinding and shrieking in the slow descent to the free-fall line, then plunging to build a new floor for the ocean—a floor of shattered glass, cement blocks, adobe, and all the rich embellishments of a palace never really earned.

Clouds of dust and explosive debris concealed the final agony of the beloved structure. Giant waves of displaced ocean swept outward again and again to lift the floating man in black and set him farther away with each rising.

And when it was done, he was grateful just to be alive and sentient.

"I actually never meant it in a literal sense," he confided to the night.

But he'd done it, yeah.

He'd shaken their damned house down.

Epilogue

"Who was that Virgin of Guadalupe," the under-boss of Pittsfield wanted to know, just for the hell of it.

"It was an inside joke, pal," replied that tired voice from the southern connection. "She was the only one in the house who wasn't for hire by the pound. Think of a virgin madam, and take it from there."

Turrin chuckled. He scratched absently at the wall of the "clear" phone booth and said, "I still sometimes don't believe you, friend. I never saw such shock waves—listen. Can you hear the screams?"

"What screams?"

"The ones echoing up and down the streets of New York. I can hear them clear from here. They lost a hell of a lot, Striker. You'd think it was the Wall Street crash, all over again. And not just with the wiseguys but with a lot of legits. It will take years to rebuild that territory. And, hell, it probably won't ever be the same."

"Let's hope not," Bolan said.

"You're okay, huh?"

"Sure. A bit travel worn and soul weary, maybe. I figure a bit of sun and sand will put it all together again."

"You're staying a while, huh?"

"Yeah. You know, Sticker . . . ?"

"Yeah?" Turrin was surprised by his grinning reflection in the phone booth. "What?"

"What's funny?"

"Aw, nothing. I'm just feeling good, I guess."

"You worry too much. Then that sets you up for too much grinning when it's all over. Save your face, Sticker."

"Go to hell, guy. What was it you were saying?"

"I was just letting the mind roll. I was thinking . . . a guy should haul his insides out from time to time, examine what's there, expose it to the fresh air."

"You're not talking about guts and stuff, I hope."

Bolan chuckled. "No. Thoughts, feelings, attitudes. That kind."

"It's too dangerous," Turrin growled. "Pandora's box, guy. Look what happened with her."

"I don't know Pandora," the big guy replied. "But there's, uh, a lot of crazy ladies down here, you know. A guy needs to reexamine his attitudes from time to time. Don't you think?"

Turrin laughed and said, "Meaning . . . ?"

"Well, times are changing. The ladies have a right, too, you know."

"Oh, sure. Absolutely. You planning on giving one her rights?"

"Let's say that I've decided to explore the question of full sexual equality."

"Liberation and all that, huh?"

"If that's what it adds up to, okay," Bolan said.

"You got, uh, someone in mind to explore it with?"

"Only about, at a quick estimate, five or six thousand."

"My God! I heard about that place but I never believed it."

"Believe it," Bolan said quietly.

"Don't get too into the, uh, faith business. It doesn't mix well with your other line of work."

"A couple of days, Sticker. Then I'll be moving on." The guy sighed a very deep one—a bone-weary one. "I'll try to post you."

"You do that."

"Thanks, guy. I couldn't have swung it without you."

"Bullshit!" Turrin growled, and hung up.

"That guy," he told his reflection in the phone booth, "could swing the world if he took a mind to."

And Leo Turrin believed that.

Yeah. He, too, was a believer.